Book 1

JEANNIE, A TEXAS FRONTIER GIRL

BY
EVELYN HORAN

AmErica House
Baltimore

First printing

ISBN: 1-58851-705-5
PUBLISHED BY AMERICA HOUSE BOOK PUBLISHERS
www.publishamerica.com
Baltimore
Printed in the United States of America

Dedication

Jeannie, A Texas Frontier Girl, Books 1, 2, 3, And 4,
Were Written For Children And Grown-Ups
Everywhere,
Who Love To Read About The Texas Frontier,

Especially For Sonny, Frances, Dianne, Richard, Mike,
Virginia, Bill, Jeannie, Bob, Desarae, Alma, Carl, Sal,
Jaime, And Joe.

For My Texas Pioneer Ancestors From Germany,
And For My Tennessee Pioneer Ancestors,
Who Migrated By Covered Wagon To Arkansas,
And On To West Texas—All, Gave Me Many Happy
Childhood Memories.

ACKNOWLEDGEMENTS

I sent my special thanks to my cousin, Patsy RS Thompson in Texas, for color illustrations of Texas flora and fauna, and to Luke Smith, a Texas rancher, in Windthorst, Texas, for his wonderful photographs of his ranch activities, and his cattle, horses, and animals. My thanks to my great-aunt Eura Pollock, who recalls much of the history of my father's family, in their early days in frontier Texas. She tells me, as a source of family pride that a Bible was given to my great-grandmother, Fanny Pollock, by her sister's child. Her niece, Pearl Buck, the well-known writer of the twenties and thirties, wrote an inscription stating something like: "To my Aunt Fanny from her loving niece, Pearl Buck."

I wish to thank my daughter Alma, Frank Quinn, and Patrick MacDonald for their help and technical assistance in computer technology. Thanks, to Carl McKay, for his illustration on my book announcements, and for the map of frontier Texas in the 1880's. I am grateful to Jeane B. Pruett, President, Central Texas, Historical & Genealogical Preservation, Inc., Museum, Ranger, Texas, for her photos of historic Ranger during its oil boom days. Finally, a thank you, to my dear friend, Jeannie Schleppe, Ranger, Texas, for her encouragement and support through the years, and for her research into Ranger's early oil history.

PREFACE

The Comanche Indians were nomadic, which means they had no permanent home. They moved about in search of food, generally following the buffalo from the Platte River in Nebraska to the Mexican border. During early frontier days, the Comanche roamed the grassy plains of Texas.

They were a proud and brave people. Their culture stressed the importance of being good warriors. They also counted their wealth by the number of horses they owned. A warrior was encouraged to steal whatever he could from other tribes.

As more and more settlers poured into Indian lands, buffalo became scarce. It was difficult for the native Americans to survive. Many were unhappy about the changing times. Some felt it was necessary to raid settlers for food and horses, and a few tried to drive the unwanted settlers out of their hunting grounds.

After a time, Indian tribes were given reservation lands by the United States government. Today, our government is sorry about the fact that it was not more considerate of the Indian and his lands during the years of expansion. It is now trying to make up for the wrongs done to the Indians in those early days when America was young.

We admire and respect the Native American nations in our country, and we appreciate their culture and their contributions to our history. But there was a time when things were different. In Texas during the late 1800's, the Comanche Indians were still feared by many settlers.

TABLE OF CONTENTS

CHAPTER PAGES

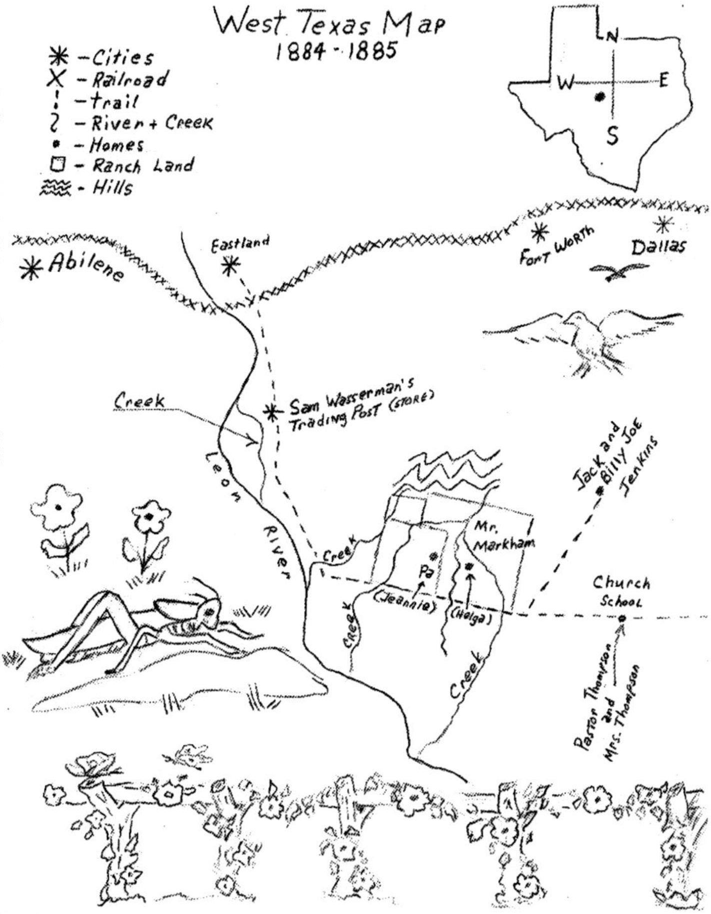

West Texas Map
1884 - 1885

✱ - Cities
X - Railroad
¦ - trail
≀ - River + Creek
• - Homes
☐ - Ranch Land
≈ - Hills

N
W
E
S

Abilene
Eastland
Fort Worth
Dallas
Creek
Sam Wasserman's Trading Post (STORE)
Leon River
Creek
Pa
(Jeannie)
Mr. Markham
(Helga)
Creek
Creek
Jack and Billy Joe Jenkins
Church School
Pastor Thompson and Mrs. Thompson

Chapter 1
"A New Colt and Plans with Pa"

West Texas Frontier
April 1884

"Jeannie, come in now," Ma called from the front porch of a wood-framed ranch house in West Texas. Shading her eyes against the late afternoon sun, she called to her daughter again, "Jeannie, supper's ready."

She tucked a wispy strand of black, wavy hair into a neatly twisted knot at the nape of her neck. As she turned to enter the house, her long, gingham dress covered by a crispy starched apron, swished around the tops of her high-buttoned shoes.

Jeannie sat perched on the top rail of the corral fence at the barn, watching some young colts frisking around the lot, playfully nipping at one another.

Hearing Ma's call, Jeannie swung a long leg down from the cedar wood fence, and with her long, yellow braids bouncing a drumbeat against her back, she raced up the narrow path to the house.

"Going to talk to Pa about that black colt," she told herself. "He sure is a pretty sight." That young stallion's tail and mane just flew in the wind like a ship's sail when he ran after his friends. Why, he looked like a big, rolling wave of black silk! Jeannie giggled softly. And the way he held his head high when he charged at the little colts - like he was already their boss! No doubt about it, he had spirit!

Two, gnarled oak trees with twisted limbs loomed above the hard-packed, red dirt of the yard. Skipping several porch steps, Jeannie leaped on the plank boards with a loud stomp. At the far end of the porch hung a swing made for two people. Beside the swing, several cane-bottomed chairs waited for an occasional visitor.

Slipping through the parlor's screened door, Jeannie dashed into her favorite, prettiest, and largest room in the house. She zoomed past Ma's prized possession, her pump organ. Ma often played church hymns on it. Sometimes, when she played and sang, the family sang along with her.

Standing in the doorway, Jeannie took a quick survey of the kitchen. She was secretly happy to find the table already set for supper. It was her chore, but Ma had done it for her. Ma knew how she felt about inside work. Once in a moment of impatience, Jeannie had exclaimed, "Ma, if I could have my 'druthers,' I'd 'druther' be outside any day, as to get 'the squirmies' sitting inside, trying to sew a quilt block or do housework and other womanly chores!"

Then Jeannie saw her mother standing with her hands on her hips. Disappointment shone in her mother's soft, brown eyes.

"Evening, Ma," Jeannie said softly.

Ma gazed at Jeannie and slowly shook her head. "Lately, dear," she said, "you're never to be found when there's work to be done in the house."

Jeannie lowered her eyes. She deserved Ma's scolding.

"Now that you're twelve years old, Jeannie—it's time to think about being a young lady instead of spending so much time down at the corral," Ma chided gently.

"Yes'm," Jeannie said. She twisted a loose strand of hair hanging about her face, like she always did, when she was nervous. "I just got so carried away watching those young colts in the corral, that I plum forgot about the time."

Sighing, Ma returned to the stove. "Hurry along now and wash up for dinner. Pa and your brother, Henry, will be here, directly."

Jeannie darted from the kitchen to the open side porch and leaned her stomach against its long, flat shelf. With a gourd dipper, she dipped water from an oaken bucket into a wash basin. Then, using a bar of homemade lye soap, she scrubbed her hands and freckled face clean, rubbed herself dry on the rough towel hanging on a nail above the shelf, and heaved the basin of used water, through the cut-away window frame, to the hard packed dirt outside.

"Howdy, Punkin," Pa said, stepping inside the back porch. His face was tired and sweaty. "Don't I look a sight, for shore?"

Although Pa was grimy with dirt, his blue eyes twinkled. He rolled up his sleeves and smiled. "I've been walking behind my hand plow, and Bessie's as tuckered out as I am." Pa shook his head affectionately. "She's a good, ole mule."

"Are you making furrows for our new cornfield?"

"Yep, Punkin." Pa filled the wash basin with water. "Soon be planting seed, now that spring's here." He gave one of Jeannie's braids a playful yank.

Giggling, she ducked and leaned against the wall.

Pa finished washing and tossed out the dirty water. Henry stepped inside the small porch next, washed, and then rubbed his sun-browned face on the towel. He reached for a comb on the shelf and pulled it quickly through his wavy, black hair.

"Y'all sit down," Ma said, wiping her hands on her apron. "Let's eat before supper gets cold."

With everyone seated around the oak table, Pa bowed his head. In a solemn, deep voice, he gave thanks to Almighty God for their many blessings. Then Ma dished up steaming plates of pinto beans and ham hocks and passed around a platter of hot cornbread.

After supper, Jeannie cleaned the dishes. Pa lit his corncob pipe and settled down in his comfortable, leather chair by the oval-shaped, stone fireplace in the parlor. Ma seated herself across from him in her rocking chair and reached inside her mending basket.

Later, Jeannie and the family's hound dog, Ole Blue, lay, side by side, near the fireplace, on Ma's multicolored rag rug. This was the time of evening Jeannie liked best. She liked to smell the sweet smell of Pa's pipe and grow drowsy listening to her parents' quiet talk.

Henry sat at the kitchen table doing his figuring by a kerosene lamp. Jeannie knew when Henry helped Pa in the fields, in the daytime, his lessons had to be done at night. Ma was firm about such things.

It was true, Henry didn't go to school anymore, since he'd gone as far as he could in Pastor Thompson's school, but Jeannie also knew Ma expected Henry to advance himself. Ma was proud of the fact she'd gone to school in Houston town. That was before she married Pa and came with him to West Texas to farm and ranch.

"I'll teach you all I know, son," Ma had said, and she was a strict teacher.

Actually, Pa wasn't much worried that Henry wasn't in school anymore. Jeannie remembered, it was about the time, when Henry turned fourteen that Pastor

Thompson told Pa he'd taken Henry as far as he could. It was in the churchyard after church, when Pastor told Pa. All Pa did was scratch his head and say, "Well, Pastor, Henry's nearly a grown man. It's about time he helped out on the farm."

Pa just shook Pastor Thompson's hand and thanked him. "Besides," Pa said, "the boy's done got more book learning than I got, and that's a fact!"

Jeannie knew Pa had only gone to the fourth grade, but even so, he didn't stop Ma from teaching Henry at home in the evenings. Jeannie sighed. As for herself, she went to school every day, but school was out this week for Easter vacation. Oh grannies! She was glad about that.

"Well, Ma, reckon, I'll hitch up and head for Wasserman's Trading Post in the morning," Pa said, rubbing his chin whiskers. "We're running low on provisions and supplies."

Jeannie stopped her daydreaming and listened. She also stopped scratching behind Ole Blue's ears. He nudged her hand with his nose and licked her face with his wet tongue.

"Reckon, you could spare my Punkin? I'd like to carry her along for company." Seeing Henry's frown, Pa added, with a nod in his son's direction, "I'd take Henry, but I want him to stay here and feed the barn animals and look after you."

Satisfied, Henry turned his attention back to his arithmetic problems.

Ma's long darning needle rose and fell on a pair of Pa's worn socks. As she waited for Ma's answer, Jeannie was positive her heart was pounding much louder than the ticking of the big grandfather clock behind Ma's rocking chair. Jeannie watched its tail wag back and forth in a steady rhythm.

Finally, Ma put the mended sock in the round wicker basket at her feet and studied Jeannie's pleading face with her steady, brown eyes. She sighed, leaned her head back on her chair, and rocked slowly. "It's awful dangerous," she said quietly, "taking a little girl in the wagon with the Comanches running wild and such."

"Aw, I'll watch out for her, Ma," Pa promised, tapping out his pipe against his ashtray. "And seeing as they ain't bother us in quite a spell, I reckon, she'll be safe enough. It's going on 1885. Most Comanches are peaceful, now."

"Well, if you think it's all right," Ma consented reluctantly, "but y'all be mighty careful."

Jeannie sprang up and threw her arms around Ma's neck in a big hug. Later, in her warm feather bed, Jeannie lay awake too excited to sleep. But soon, she felt a gentle touch on her shoulders.

"Get up, honey," Ma whispered softly. "You want to be ready when Pa gets back from the barn where he's hitching up."

Springing out of bed, Jeannie dressed quickly by lamplight. Hurriedly, she splashed her face with cold water from the basin on the back porch and sat down to a breakfast of biscuits and milk gravy with pork sausage.

When Pa pulled up in the wagon, Jeannie gulped down her last bite of biscuit, and raced outside to greet the early morning sun, peeking above the purple hills in the east. She climbed up beside Pa and leaned over the wagon seat for the basket Ma had packed for their noontime dinner. While she was eating her breakfast, she had watched Ma put in a jar of buttermilk, pieces of cold chicken, and tasty biscuits filled with molasses.

"I'll try and get back before too late," Pa said. "So don't worry none, Ma."

"Well, reckon, I'll worry a mite," Ma said, nervously putting her hands in and out of her apron pockets. "Do you have your rifle?"

"Yes, Ma," Pa reassured, "but I won't have to use it."

Ma gave him a worried look and said, "I surely hope not." She shielded her forehead with her hands, shading her eyes against the bright, morning sunlight. "Do you have the list of things we need?"

"Yep." Pa patted his vest pocket.

Ma studied the ground for a moment. "I wonder if there is anything else I should tell you...."

"Now, Ma, we'll be back before dark," Pa said. He reached down and kissed his wife goodbye. "Get along there Bessie!" Pa ordered. "Ho there, Jake!" He shook the mules' reins, and the wagon creaked away.

"Goodbye, y'all be careful," Ma called. "Be a good girl, Jeannie."

"I will, Ma." Jeannie leaned around the high spring-seat of the wagon and waved a cheery goodbye. Oh, grannies! It was going to be a wonderful day. She just knew it!

Chapter 2
"A Narrow Escape"

The sun shone brightly overhead. Jeannie brushed her damp bangs away from her forehead, just as the wagon came to a stop beside Wasserman's General Store in the trading post settlement. Then she jumped down and followed Pa into the store.

For a time, Jeannie listened to him and other men talk about the way the settlement was filling up with new folks, and how, one of these days, there might even be a railroad coming through. Then, tiring of "menfolks' talk," she wandered happily around the store, looking at all the interesting items for sale, sucking on a red, peppermint candy cane, Mr. Wasserman had given her.

On the way home, Pa asked, "Well, Punkin, did you have a good time?"

"Yep," Jeannie said, smiling happily, as she watched a butterfly flitting around Bessie's ear. "Mr. Wasserman's sure got a lot of pretty things in his store." The wagon bounced bumpily over pebbles on the dirt trail. "It'd probably take a million dollars to buy everything in there."

"Hmm, could be," Pa said softly. Through squinted eyes, he studied a distant dust cloud. "I allow that to be about three or four horsemen." His voice was low. "Could be Injuns--reckon it is--it is for a fact! Hurry," he said sharply. "Get under the wagon seat."

Jeannie crouched under the seat, and Pa covered her with a bright piece of calico. He was bringing it home for Ma to sew herself a new dress. "And here's an old toe-sack," Pa said, putting a brown, coarsely woven feed bag over the calico material.

"Now, lay real still," he warned. "I've heard tell

that sometimes Injuns like to take little girls and raise them up Comanche. They're right partial to blonde ones, too! So, say a little prayer, Punkin. Ask the good Lord to help us."

Jeannie closed her eyes and prayed without making a sound.

Whistling softly, Pa put his rifle down at his feet and pushed his legs tight against the wagon's front boards.

Underneath the calico covering, between Pa's legs, Jeannie peeked through the sideboards. Several Indians, wearing loincloth around their waists, approached on their ponies. Their bronze-colored bodies were decorated with bright paint, and they wore beaded moccasins on their feet. A tall Indian lifted his right arm at the elbow, with his flattened palm upward, in a greeting of peace.

Pa stopped the wagon, lifted his arm in a similar show of friendship, and asked, "What can I do for you?"

"You got sugar?"

"No, no sugar," Pa said.

The leader signaled his two companions to examine the wagon. One moved packages and parcels around in the back, while the other, heavier Indian brave drew his pony in closer to Pa. Seeing bits of the colored cloth underneath the wagon seat, he leaned over to examine it.

Pa sat still. The toe of his boot touched his rifle barrel.

The Indian brave reached down for the calico material, but the leader gave an impatient command and motioned to his companions. They wheeled their ponies off the trail and rode away in a heavy cloud of dust.

When they were out of sight, Pa lifted the calico material and asked, "How are you doing, Punkin? Did you ask God to help us?"

"I sure did, Pa." Jeannie's voice shook. "I asked Him to please help us out of this one." She stared wide-eyed into the distance beyond the wagon. "God is always there, when we need Him, isn't He, Pa?"

"You bet," Pa said. "You can see, He answered your prayer. The Injuns are gone." Pa gave the reins a shake, and the wagon lurched forward. "Yep, you can always count on Him to help you out, when you're in a tight squeeze."

Jeannie straightened up, her yellow hair mussed and tangled. "Just wait until I tell Ma and Henry about this one!" she exclaimed.

The sun was setting in a burst of deep oranges and reds behind the purple foothills, when Pa pulled their dusty wagon to a stop before the wooden porch steps of their ranch house. Inside, they both knew they would find Ma's comforting arms, some warm food, and plenty of love waiting for them.

Chapter 3
"Indian Rustlers"

A few days later, smiling happily at the supper table, Pa announced, "Them young colts are almost grown, and some will fetch a good selling price in Fort Worth."

After supper, he and Jeannie strolled down to the corral, while Henry worked on his lessons. Jeannie perched on the top fence rail, and Pa lit his pipe and stepped up beside her. They sat watching the colts frisking about the corral.

Then Jeannie nudged Pa and said, "Look at that black one over there. Watch how he tries to boss all the others by running up and biting them on their rumps."

Suddenly, the young stallion left his playmates and charged down the corral toward Jeannie. His jet coat shone in the last rays of sunlight, as his long mane streamed out behind him. He slid to an abrupt stop a few yards from her, and stared wide-eyed, with his nostrils blowing and flaring.

Jeannie sat frozen, unable to move. He was so beautiful!

Then the colt tossed his head and raced back to his friends.

"Oh, Pa," Jeannie whispered. "I want that colt. I'd like to try to tame him, so I could ride him."

"Now, hold on, Punkin," Pa said. "You know I'd give you most anything, but that little stallion is a real, feisty one. He won't even let me get near him."

"But, I know, he'd let me, Pa," Jeannie coaxed. "Please, Pa." Jeannie leaned her head on Pa's shoulders and gazed up at him. Love shone in her blue eyes.

"Well, all right," Pa said reluctantly. "I reckon so."

Jeannie knew it was hard for Pa to refuse her most

anything.

"But you better not hurt yourself, or your Ma will skin us both alive!"

"Thanks, Pa," Jeannie squealed. She threw her arms around Pa's neck and kissed his cheek. Laughing, they both reached wildly for the fence railing to recover their lost balance.

Each day after school, Jeannie hurried to the pasture where Pa had put the horses to graze. She whistled to attract the young stallion's attention. Finally, with quivering lips, he drew near and reached for the lump of sugar in her outstretched palm.

As the days passed, he seemed to expect Jeannie's low, soft whistle. When he saw her, he pricked up his ears and stepped closer for the lump of sugar that was always in her hand.

"I'm going to call you, Diamond," Jeannie whispered, as he nibbled the sugar from her palm. "You've got the prettiest white, diamond-shaped hair, right there, in the middle of your forehead." She gently caressed the area.

One warm day in early May, Jeannie walked to the meadow as usual, but this time, she held a bridle. She whistled, and Diamond obediently trotted close for his sugar lump. He stood still and allowed her to stroke his neck and pet his face.

"Whoa, boy." Jeannie spoke in a low, soothing voice. "See this bridle. It won't hurt you." Carefully, she slipped the bridle over Diamond's head, and pulled on the reins gently, ever so gently, coaxing him forward.

Jeannie led Diamond around the pasture several times and stopped at the fence. Then she stepped on the highest wood railing, threw one leg over Diamond, and plopped on his back. He snorted in surprise, and away they flew!

Diamond ran, jumped, tossed his head, reeled, and kicked up his hind legs, trying to unseat his uncomfortable burden, but Jeannie gritted her teeth and gathered the reins in tighter. Suddenly, Diamond snorted and heaved hard, tossing her face down in the soft, prairie grass.

The bridle reins dangled between his legs as he trotted away. Jeannie lay panting on the ground, among the scarlet Indian paintbrushes and Texas blue bonnets -- too dazed to move. Slowly, she turned on her side and propped herself up on an elbow.

"Mister, if you ain't the most ungrateful horse!" she shouted angrily, rubbing her sore nose. "I come all the way out here, bring you sugar, feed you, and ... and ...." She ran out of breath. "Oh! You just wait. I'll ride you yet!"

Jeannie rose slowly. The earth reeled about her, and every muscle in her body ached. "Well," she consoled herself, "I rode him for a few minutes, anyway. If I rode him once, I can do it again." Feeling stiff and sore, but determined, she limped her way out of the pasture.

Although school ended for summer vacation the second week in May, and Jeannie had more time to work with the colt, she sometimes wondered why she didn't give up the whole, impossible idea. Her muscles ached. She dragged herself home every evening. But rested, by morning, she tried again.

Finally, Diamond surrendered. He quieted down and let her ride him. Then they loped around the pasture, in an easy canter, with Jeannie's blonde braids flying, and Diamond's tail streaming out behind him.

Sitting on Diamond's muscular back, rising and falling in graceful tempo, with the rhythmic pounding of his hoofs, Jeannie smiled to herself. It was just like sitting in Ma's rocking chair. It was a wonderful ride!

Late one night, Jeannie awoke to hear confused tramping of horses and their whinnying cries of fright. She threw back the covers and raced to the window. As she peered out, her stomach tightened with fear.

She could see painted figures astride horses in the bright moonlight. They were waving their arms and urging the stolen horses south toward the cedar woods along the Leon River.

Diamond struggled against a huge Indian, who beat him with a stick and kicked him. "Oh, no!" Jeannie moaned helplessly. "Don't hit Diamond!"

The brave held a rope around Diamond's neck and was forcing him to follow his pony.

Ma entered the room, white-faced and tense. "Some Indians are rustling the horses," she whispered. "Don't stand in from of the window, dear."

"They're taking Diamond," Jeannie wailed, tearfully plopping herself down on her bed.

"I'm so sorry, Jeannie," Ma said gently. She placed a comforting arm on Jeannie's shoulders. "Try not to worry. Pa's gone after them. He sent Henry over to Mr. Markham's ranch to get help." She sighed and hugged Jeannie close. "Go back to bed, dear. There's nothing we can do now, but wait."

Chapter 4
"Jeannie Follows"

After Ma left the room, Jeannie rummaged through her oak dresser drawers and pulled out a pair of overalls. Her heart pounded with excitement and guilt. She'd have to face Ma later on. What would she say when Ma found out? Well, she couldn't think about that. She had to go through with it now. She climbed into her overalls, tucked her gown inside, and slipped on her boots. She had to hurry to catch up with Pa.

Jeannie crept silently to the parlor door. Cautiously, she let herself out into the yard and sprinted for the corral. The cool wind blew across her face, making her wide-awake.

She peered inside the barn. "Good! Comanches left Bessie. Probably didn't want a mule. Too slow for them," she told herself.

She found a bridle and slipped the bit in Bessie's mouth. There was no time for a saddle. She threw a saddle blanket over Bessie's back, mounted, and gave a little kick to Bessie's side.

Following on the wagon trail, Jeannie guided Bessie, among the shadowy cedars, toward the Leon River. She tried to avoid the bright moonlight. The last thing she wanted was to be seen.

Where were the ranch hands? And where was Pa? Maybe she shouldn't have just left on her own like this. Ma would be madder than a wet hen, and who knows, what Pa would say or do when he saw her? Maybe she should just turn back.

From a heavy clump of shrubbery, a low voice hissed, "Jeannie! Come here!"

Jeannie froze and jerked back on Bessie's reins.

Pa sat on his horse glaring at her. “And just what are you doing here, little girl?” he demanded tersely, looking ready to explode.

“I came after Diamond, Pa,” Jeannie said meekly. She reached for a loose strand of hair and twisted it around her finger.

Pa gave her a stony stare and shook his head. “Sometimes, I can’t make heads or tails out of you, Punkin -- Of all the dingblasted, confounded stunts you’ve pulled -- this beat them all, for sure!”

Grannies! Jeannie knew she was in big trouble. That was a mouthful coming from Pa. She hung her head low and waited.

Pa prodded his horse so hard he jumped forward. “Whoa, Smokey,” Pa said. “Well, if you’re coming with me,” he called over his shoulder, “you’d better get started.”

Jeannie rode up beside Pa. She gave him a quick glance from the corner of her eye. Pa was grim-faced and silent. When he turned her way, she glanced at him again and ventured a weak smile.

Pa glared back and tugged at his beard for a few seconds. Then he shook his head, grinned a little, and reached over and yanked on her braid.

Jeannie took a deep breath. She was forgiven. Everything was all right for the moment. But there was still Ma. Jeannie shook her head. She couldn’t think about that now.

A short time later, Jeannie and Pa lay on their stomachs, behind a thicket of wild shrubbery, near the Leon River.

“From what I can see,” Pa whispered, “it looks like

the Comanches are feeling pretty safe. They camped on this side of the river. They're just sitting in a circle around a campfire laughing and talking."

"They're probably talking about how easy it was to take our horses," Jeannie muttered. She stared at the dark shapes of their stolen horses tied to the distant trees.

"Punkin, to a Comanche's way of thinking, stealing horses is a thing to do," Pa explained softly. "They don't see no wrong in it. Taking horses is a sign of courage, and it's a way they figure out a warrior's wealth--by how many horses he owns."

"Well, they can't have my Diamond!" Jeannie whispered back.

Slowly, one by one, the Indians drifted off to sleep.

Pa pulled out his round pocket watch. "It's 1:30 A.M.," he said, studying its hands. "Them cow punchers ought to be here about now." He tucked the watch back into his vest pocket.

Jeannie's legs ached from their cramped position. "I sure hope they get here soon," she murmured.

Something was creeping through the undergrowth behind them. Pa waited with pistol drawn. The bushes parted. Pa's fingers tightened on the trigger. Then Henry stumbled in.

"Pa!" he whispered. "I came this way looking for you."

Pa holstered his revolver and put his forefinger to his lips. "Shh," he said. Crouching, they backed away to an oak tree where their mounts waited.

"Glad to see you, son," Pa said, standing. He patted Henry's shoulder. "Are the men with you?"

"Yep," Henry said quickly. "We rode south from

Mr. Markham's ranch. I told them, the Indians were traveling through the cedar woods toward the river."

"Good. Where's your horse?"

"I left Scout with the men back yonder behind those big rocks." Henry pointed to a denser part of the cedar woods. "You told me to meet you at the river, so I came to find you."

"That's good," Pa said. "The Comanches are camped down there, just like I figured they might be, probably thinking no one is following them."

Henry glared down at Jeannie. With a jerk of his head, he asked, "What's she doing here?"

"Never mind that now, son," Pa said, mounting Smokey.

As Jeannie climbed up on Bessie, she shot a dark look at Henry.

"Let's go find Mr. Markham," Pa said.

Chapter 5
"Will Pa's Plan work?"

Riding slowly, Jeannie and Pa followed Henry, who trudged ahead on foot. He led them a short distance east of the river. He wound through oak trees and cedars, leading them through heavy chaparral until they reached a large, rock boulder where men were waiting.

"Howdy, Frank," Pa said dismounting. He shook hands with his tall friend. "Thanks for coming."

"We're here to help, Matthew," Frank Markham said.

"Howdy, boys," Pa said. He exchanged quiet greetings with Mr. Markham's cowboys. "Glad you could come." Pa gestured over his shoulder. "Them Injuns are all sleeping around a campfire, about a hundred yards back yonder. Lucky for us, they're on this side of the river." Several cowboys nodded.

Pa went on, "They have our horses tied to a single rope line. That rope is tied around a big cedar tree near their campfire. Now, the hard part is to get past the Injuns and cut this line free, without waking them. They might not be sleeping very sound."

"That's a fact," Mr. Markham agreed.

"To get the job done, I reckon it'll take four of us," Pa said, as the men listened and waited. "The rest can stay here and give us cover when we start back."

Pa looked at Henry. "Son," he said, "you stay and help reload rifles and pistols when the shooting starts."

Henry's shoulders slumped. Jeannie knew Henry would like to go with Pa, but he didn't argue. He just nodded and hung his head. Jeannie figured Henry was probably hoping to carry a rifle and help out that way, but she could see Pa wasn't ready for him to do that. Not by a long shot! Sure, Henry was allowed to go rabbit and squirrel hunting. And he'd even gone deer hunting in the woods with Pa.

Jeannie remembered back to the time last winter when Pa and Henry had come home with a big buck they'd killed for food, but she couldn't eat any of it. Instead, she'd just felt sorry for the buck. She couldn't help it. She dearly loved all helpless critters.

And now, every time she walked into the parlor and looked on the wall, near the fireplace, she saw that poor buck's head! First thing Pa did was stuff it. He even took pride in having it hanging up there. Sometimes, it was hard to figure out the ways of menfolks.

A hoot owl hooted, lonesome-like, in a tree, somewhere behind them. Pa glanced around at the cowboys. "Anybody volunteer to go with me?" he asked.

"I'll go," a tall cowboy said.

"Thanks, Slim," Pa said.

"Count me in," another said.

"Grateful, Waco," Pa said, with a nod of appreciation.

"Let me go too, Pa," Jeannie said.

"Now, you stay out of this, Punkin," Pa said.

"But, Pa, I'm little, and I can crawl good," Jeannie whispered. "It wouldn't be hard for me. And they've got Diamond." She tried to keep her voice from shaking. "I'm little and fast. I can get the job done in a hurry."

"All right," Pa relented with a sigh, "but you'll stay close to me."

Pa squatted on the ground and sketched a map in the dirt with his forefinger. "When we get back to where we was watching the Comanches, we start crawling."

As the group squatted around the drawing, Henry cupped a lighted match in his hands and said, "This will help us see better."

"Be careful with that light, son," Pa cautioned gently. "Don't want them Injuns to see it." Then, he put an "X" at the spot where he and Jeannie had watched the Indian camp. Next, he drew a line for the river and put an "X" for the sleeping Indians.

"Now, we'll circle around them until we come to where the horses are tied." He made a half circle north and a half circle south of the "X" representing the sleeping Indians.

"The horses are all tied to one guideline, so we'll cut that rope and lead them straight back here," Pa said. "If the Injuns wake up when we start leading the broncos away," he said, looking at Slim and Waco, "y'all keep us covered from yore end."

Both men nodded.

"And you," he looked Jeannie square in the eyes, "you stick to me like glue, Punkin."

"Yes, Pa," Jeannie whispered.

"Matthew, we'll be here, giving you cover, in case they follow you," Mr. Markham said, checking his rifle.

"Thanks," Pa said, with a grateful nod.

Waco and Slim examined their pistols and adjusted their cartridge belts. Then the small group crept forward slowly in opposite directions. When the Indians' camp came in view, all four stretched flat on their stomachs. Jeannie and Pa moved south of the camp, and the cowboys circled north of it.

Jeannie held Pa's jack knife in her hand. It felt cool and sharp. A moment ago, he'd reached in his pocket and given it to her. Pa was holding the long bowie knife he always carried in his saddlebags.

They crawled along silently, turning in toward the camp. Soon, they saw the painted, bronzed faces of the sleeping Indians. Jeannie's heart leaped in her throat. She could almost reach out and touch one of them.

A loud crack sounded! Jeannie gasped. "Oh, dear Lord, help me," she murmured. "I crawled over a dry branch and broke it."

The sleeping Indian muttered and rolled over on his side. Jeannie closed her eyes and whispered, "Thank You, God. Thank You."

Finally, they reached their horses and rose up carefully. Jeannie's knees wobbled. Pa reached out to steady her. Then he pointed to the thick, rawhide rope tied around the tree trunk just above her head. Jeannie gripped it tightly and sawed at its knotted ends with the pocketknife. Pa moved slowly, holding onto the rope, as he crept to its far end where the horses were tied.

Still, all was quiet. With one slash, Pa severed the rest of the guide rope and cut Diamond free from the others. Jeannie crept close to Pa. She patted Diamond's neck and reached to cover his nostrils. Too late! He nickered softly.

The sound roused the big Indian. He sprang to his knees with a loud cry of alarm. His drowsy companions awakened and groped for their rifles.

"Come, Jeannie!" Pa commanded. In one swift

movement, he mounted Diamond. He held the guide rope of the other horses in his left hand. Reaching down, with his free hand, Pa lifted Jeannie up in front of him.

"Hold on tight," Pa said. "These are the same Injuns that stopped us when we was coming home from the trading post. I remember the big one." Pa kicked Diamond hard in his sides, and the stallion shot off in a fast gallop.

Bullets whined past to lodge in tree trunks and low-hanging branches as they raced by. Pa headed southeast toward the rock boulder. From the north, Slim and Waco fired on the Comanches. At the rock boulder, Mr. Markham and his cowboys opened fire on the angry Indians, who had mounted their ponies and were now following Pa and Jeannie in fast pursuit.

But the confused Comanches soon realized they were being attacked from several sides. They wheeled their ponies and turned back. The loud clattering of their horses' hooves splashed the river's shallow water, as the outnumbered Indians frantically raced to safety on the west side of the river.

The woods quieted down, about the time Jeannie and Pa drew up beside the rock boulder. After quickly glancing around at the others, and watching, as Slim and Waco brought their mounts to a halt, Pa turned and said, "Well, Frank, it looks like we're all here, and we're all okay–so, I reckon, it's time we headed on back to the ranch to get some sleep."

"Reckon so," Mr. Markham agreed, returning his rifle to its saddle holster. "Time to get some shut eye. There's branding to do in the morning."

"Well, you boys know how much obliged I am

for all yore help," Pa said gratefully, reaching over and shaking each man's hand.

When the trail reached the Markham ranch gate, the cowboy called Slim, rode up close to Jeannie and patted her shoulder. Then he put his forefinger to his hat brim in a friendly, goodbye salute. "You sure are a mighty, spunky little lady," he said.

Jeannie smiled and murmured. "Thanks. I knew I was safe with my Pa."

Later, when Diamond and the other recaptured horses were inside the corral, Jeannie put her arms around Diamond's neck and whispered, "God is so good! He gave you back to me, and now you're mine, all mine, forever and ever."

Diamond nickered softly, as if to say, "I'm glad I'm home."

Chapter 6
"Facing Up to Ma"

Was that the sweet smell of salt pork frying? Yawning noisily, Jeannie turned and blinked at the bright, morning sunlight streaming in her bedroom window. Little dust flecks danced in its rays.

"You awake, Jeannie?" Ma called from the kitchen. "Hurry and get dressed, sleepyhead. I've warmed your breakfast for you. It's almost time for me to fix Pa's noontime dinner."

"Getting up now," Jeannie called back, slipping into her overalls and boots. In the parlor, the black hands of the grandfather clock pointed to ten. Jeannie gasped. She'd slept away most of the morning!

"Sit down and eat, dear," Ma said, giving Jeannie a warm plate of food.

Breakfast tasted wonderful! Bacon and eggs with a sweetener -- sorghum molasses mixed in butter and sopped up with hunks of thick biscuits.

"Are you all slept out?" Ma asked. She sat across from Jeannie and sipped her coffee.

Jeannie nodded, finishing her breakfast. Ma was looking at her with one of her gentle stares. "Is there anything you want to tell me, dear?" she asked.

A sharp twinge of guilt stabbed Jeannie's chest! The last bite of biscuit tasted like dried hay, but she slowly choked it down. She couldn't look at her mother. "I'm sorry, Ma," she whispered, choking back tears. "They took Diamond. Ma, I just had to help get him back."

"Jeannie, Jeannie," Ma chided softly, with a heavy sigh. "You're a girl. You're supposed to be a young lady. Last night was man's work."

"I know, Ma."

"And you left without telling me."

Jeannie nodded, as a tear rolled down her cheek.

"And worst of all, you could have been hurt. I was so worried."

"I'm sorry, Ma," Jeannie sobbed. "I was just thinking about Diamond."

Ma rose, rubbing her hands on her apron. "What am I going to do with you, Jeannie?"

"Please forgive me, Ma," Jeannie said, twisting a loose strand of hair around her finger. "It won't ever happen again."

"You could have been hurt bad, real bad," Ma said. Her voice caught on a sob.

Jeannie leaped up and hugged Ma tightly around her waist and pressed her face against Ma's bosom. "Don't cry, Ma, please. I'll never do it again."

Ma wiped her eyes on her apron and kissed Jeannie's forehead. "Is that a promise?" she asked, tilting Jeannie's chin and looking her straight in the eyes.

Quickly running her finger across her chest, Jeannie said, "Yes'm, I cross my heart and hope to die, if I am telling a lie."

Ma smiled and said, "That's not necessary."

"Well," Jeannie said solemnly, "I promise, never again."

Henry stepped on the back porch and scooped a dipper of water from the oaken bucket. "Hey Shorty," he called in the doorway, "want to come with me? Pa said he didn't need me for the rest of the day."

"Do you need me, Ma?" Jeannie asked.

"No, dear, I'm going to fix Pa's dinner. Go with Henry if you want to."

"Thanks, Ma," Jeannie said, hurrying down the back porch steps with Henry. Ole Blue followed, wagging his tail and sniffing the air.

The June sun shone brightly on yellow primroses blooming in the back yard. As they circled around to the front of the house, Henry squinted up at the sky. "We're in for some hot weather this summer," he said. "You can mark my word on it."

"I like hot weather," Jeannie said.

Strolling toward the barnyard, they paused at the pigpen's gray-planked fence. They watched a mother sow and her squealing, little piglets. They crowded around her short, fat legs, nudging noisily against her full teats, and making loud, sucking sounds.

"They sure are hungry," Jeannie said, laughing at their greediness. She held her nose. "Phew-EE!" The muddy pigpen smelled of slop and pig dung. "Let's get out of here!" she cried. "Look, Henry, even Ole Blue is brushing his nose with his paws."

Hurrying beyond the fence, they paused to watch Ma's chickens, scratching at pieces of dried hay in the barnyard lot.

"Soo, Lu-Lu, soo," Jeannie called softly to their milk cow. Lu-Lu stood in the shade of a live oak tree nearby. She flicked an ear, swished her tail across her bony back, and continued chewing on her cud. Ole Blue barked several times, but Lu-Lu ignored him.

"Let's go to the haystack," Jeannie said. "I feel like sliding down it."

"That's for young'uns," Henry said, stuffing his hands inside the pockets of his overalls.

"Oh, come on, Henry," Jeannie coaxed. "Don't be

an old stick in the mud! It'll be fun." She trotted behind the barn to the dried haystack near the fence.

Henry followed reluctantly.

Struggling upward, Jeannie dug her fingers into the loose strands of yellow hay, searching for a solid pack. She and Henry reached the top of the hay at the same time.

"Okay, let's go!" Jeannie cried. "Yah-hoo!" she screamed. The cool breeze fanned her face, as she slithered down the dried haystack. "Get out of the way, Ole Blue!" Jeannie called, before she crashed into him at the bottom. Blue barked and wagged his tail playfully.

"One more time," Jeannie said, climbing back up the stack.

Turkey hens, scratching in the loose hay at the base of the stack, fluttered their wings and cocked beaded eyes, as Henry and Jeannie tore down the stack once more.

This time Henry yelled along with her. "Yippee!" he shouted, zipping down the stack and landing on his feet.

All this excitement caused Ole Blue to dance around and chase the turkey hens. Jeannie knew Ma wouldn't like that. "Stop it, Blue," she called. "Settle down. Get over here!"

Henry dusted straw from Jeannie's back. "I'm going to the house for a minute, Shorty. I want to get my shotgun. I'm gonna shoot me a jack rabbit," he said, jogging away. "Start walking," he called over his shoulder. "I'll catch up."

Jeannie wasn't much excited about going rabbit hunting with Henry. Still, there were a lot of those ornery critters all over their place, always bothering Ma's vegetable garden and eating her fresh vegetables. Jeannie guessed it would be all right for Henry to get rid of a few.

She strolled toward the east pasture, breathing in the sweet-smelling June air. How she dearly loved the openness of easy, rolling flatlands! It felt good to be outdoors. Here and there, bright blue, Texas bluebonnets and scarlet Indian paintbrushes added color.

"God sure made a pretty world," she said when Henry caught up with her.

"That's a fact!" Henry agreed. They ambled leisurely along, stepping across small rocks and over tiny, round clumps of brush. Tall, yellow sunflowers and clusters of prairie zinnias bowed their heads gracefully in the occasional breeze.

Jeannie blinked as a fat, green grasshopper darted past her face to settle in a patch of gray weeds. Ole Blue jumped at it, and chased it for a time, but he returned without catching the bothersome insect.

"Let's see if the creek still has some water," Henry said. "It's a little late in the morning, but we might see a jack rabbit getting a drink, if we hurry."

"Okay," Jeannie said, scooping up a stone and sailing it out high in the air.

Henry inhaled and sucked in his lower lip. Then he curled his tongue over, made a slight funnel with it, and blew out a loud, shrill, whistle-sound, piercing the morning stillness.

"Jumping Jupiter, Henry! How'd you do that?" Jeannie asked. "I've tried and tried, but I can't make that kind of whistle sound."

"Aw, it's easy," Henry said, kicking a dried stick from his path.

Jeannie stopped, inhaled, tightened her lower lip, curled her tongue over, and blew. "See!" she cried, shaking her head in disgust. "Nothing happened!"

"Here, like this," Henry said, patiently stooping down, eye to eye with her. "Watch me." He formed his lips and tongue slowly and gave a few, short, low whistles.

Jeannie tried and tried. She blew soft air until her face turned red.

Chuckling, Henry yanked one of her braids and said, "Just got to keep practicing, Shorty." He dashed off with Ole Blue close at his heels, before Jeannie had time to sock him back.

Chapter 7
"Going Hunting and Meeting New Friends"

They walked on until they reached the barbed wire fence separating their land from Mr. Markham's land. Thrusting a heavy boot on the lower wire, Henry held it down taunt, lifted the top wire, and stretched it up, allowing space for Jeannie to bend down and step through without snagging herself. Then she did the same for him, while she listened to a killdeer on a nearby fence post calling to its mate.

Soon, standing on a grassy knoll, and looking beyond for a short distance, they saw the winding creek, slicing through Mr. Markham's rolling pasture.

"Yes, sir-ee bob!" Henry exclaimed, slapping his thigh. "Creek's got water. I hear it running."

He trotted off with Jeannie following close behind. There it was, not more than eight feet wide, bending and curling along--its shallow, muddy water flowing at a steady rate. They followed the bank's shoulder until it narrowed down to a few yards in width.

"Might as well leave my rifle here," Henry said, putting his gun on a flat rock. "I'll get it later on our way back. Don't see any rabbits, anyhow."

He stretched his long legs for the jump across, and landed upright, with his feet together. Ole Blue followed. "Come on over, Shorty," Henry said, waiting with his hands on his hips. "You can do it."

Hoping she wouldn't fall in and embarrass herself, Jeannie backed up for a running leap. She soared through the air, over the water, and landed beside Henry. He reached out and steadied her.

"You made it, Shorty!" he shouted, pounding her on the back.

"Of course," Jeannie said, swaggering a bit. "It was easy. Wasn't nothing, but a bird nest on the ground!" However, her heart was beating so fast, it felt like it would jump out of her chest.

Beyond a grove of oak trees, they glimpsed Mr. Markham's ranch house. A hound dog waited on the front porch, with its ears cocked, watching them, and barking loudly.

"Let's go," Henry said. "Lady's barking and carrying on, like we're a couple of rustlers stalking the place. They've seen us, by now."

The porch screened door opened. An attractive woman with blonde braids circling her head, smiled and waited, as they approached. "Hush that barking, Lady. Good afternoon, kinder, (children)," she said.

"Howdy," Henry said. Ole Blue and Lady touched noses and sniffed at one another. "We're your neighbors from the ranch over there," Henry said, pointing west.

"Ach ja, (oh yes), I'm Frau (Mrs.) Lengenfeld, Mr. Markham's new housekeeper."

"Pleased to meet you," Henry said, taking off his hat and holding it in his hands. "This is my sister, Jeannie."

Mrs. Lengenfeld smiled and nodded. "I don't speak, so goot English," she said. "Ve are new to Texas from Germany," she continued. "I write Mr. Markham letter. I see newspaper notice in Germany. He needs cook and housekeeper on big ranch. Many years ago, my husband pass away, so I tink is good idea to come to America."

"Well, I hope you like it in Texas," Henry said, smiling.

"Ja, ja. Is big country. Ve get here last veek," Mrs.

Lengenfeld said, wiping her hands on her apron. "You vant some coffee cake and milk?"

Henry glanced at Jeannie. She smiled and nodded.

"Yes'm, thank you," Henry said. "Be a good dog, Blue." Henry patted Ole Blue's head and said, "Don't be playing rough with your friend, Lady. She's a hound dog, but she's a lot smaller than you."

"Come, ve go to kitchen," Mrs. Lengenfeld said, leading the way through a spacious parlor.

A girl, about Jeannie's age, sat near the round oak table in the kitchen. She was working a plunger up and down in a butter churn.

Her hair is pretty like cotton, Jeannie thought. And her eyes are sky-blue. But her skin is as white as the milk she's churning into butter. Poor little thing. She could use some sun.

"Dis is mine daughter, Helga. Say, 'Goot day,' Helga."

"Goot day," Helga said shyly, biting her lower lip.

"Howdy," Jeannie said. "My name's Jeannie, and this is my brother, Henry."

Helga smiled and nodded.

"Sit," Mrs. Lengenfeld said, setting two, large glasses of milk and two, fat slices of cake before them. "I make goot coffee cake," she said.

Returning home, Jeannie paused at a stand of tall, yellow sunflowers and a clump of baby blue eyes. She gave Henry the coffeecake Mrs. Lengenfeld had sent to Ma.

"I'll take Ma a bunch of these sunflowers," Jeannie said. "They'll look pretty on the kitchen table. Carry the cake and don't drop it."

Henry sighed. "Shorty, you're bossy!" he said. "I won't drop it."

"Mrs. Lengenfeld said, to tell Ma, she wants to meet her soon."

"Unhuh, I heard her say that, too."

Jeannie was careful to select long-stemmed sunflowers. They would look pretty, standing tall in Ma's fruit jar.

"Helga's going to school in September," Jeannie said, admiring her bouquet. "She'll soon be twelve, like me, so she'll probably sit near me."

"I reckon," Henry said in a bored voice. "Sure am glad, I'm through with school." He kicked at a stone in his path as they walked on. "Besides, Pa only went to the fourth grade. I made it through the eighth grade. Pa says I got a good enough schooling for farming and ranching."

"Well, that's as far as Pastor Thompson could take you, anyway," Jeannie said. "Ma says we're fortunate to have him to do the Lord's work on Sunday, and then, teach us children lessons during the school year."

Sprawled on a flat rock, near the sunflowers, a horned toad stared back at them. Ole Blue stiffened with his tail pointing straight out.

"Ma says you still have to work on your ciphering," Jeannie reminded, watching the toad. "Guess you know, Ma's some better at it than Pastor Thompson."

"Yeah, well, don't tell Pastor that," Henry said. "Sic him, Blue, get that horned toad. Sic him!" Henry hissed loudly.

Ole Blue leaped for the horned toad, but the toad was too fast. He slithered down the backside of the rock and slipped underneath. Ole Blue growled and scratched in the warm dirt around the rock, whining and sniffing in confused frustration.

"Leave him be, Blue," Jeannie said. "Let's go."

Reluctantly, Ole Blue followed, glancing back, once or twice.

"I think Ma will like Mrs. Lengenfeld," Jeannie said. "Be nice for her to have a lady friend on the next ranch. Ever since Mrs. Markham died last year, Ma's been lonely for woman talk."

Henry nodded.

"Don't drop the cake," Jeannie reminded again, as they approached the creek.

"I told you, I won't," Henry said, holding the cake carefully. He took one long leap, followed by Ole Blue. He was once again standing on the other side of the water.

Jeannie backed up to get a running start. This time, she crossed and landed upright on her feet.

"Good jump, Shorty!" Henry said, shifting the cake to his other hand. With his free hand, he gave Jeannie's back an enthusiastic pat, almost pushing her over.

"Hey!" Jeannie cried. "Not so hard!" She doubled up her fist and raised the knuckle on her middle finger, hoping for a bigger impact, when she poked her brother's shoulder, but it didn't seem to faze Henry. He only grinned, picked up his rifle, and continued walking.

Ole Blue ran ahead, as usual. Suddenly, he stopped and stiffened. A few yards beyond, two, long ears were sticking up in the prairie grass. Henry quickly threw an arm across Jeannie's stomach. It almost took her breath away, when he halted her pace. Giving her the cake, Henry raised his rifle, and took aim.

Cautiously, the jackrabbit poked his head up. Ole

Blue barked, and the rabbit took off in a zigzag path to the left. Henry's rifle barrel followed, as he sighted in on the rabbit. Then Henry squeezed the trigger, and the rabbit disappeared in the tall grass. "Go get him, Blue," Henry called.

Jeannie didn't have to wonder about it long. Sure enough, in a few moments, there was Ole Blue trotting back, holding a dead jackrabbit in his mouth.

"Got him in the head," Henry said, with a satisfied grin. He took the jackrabbit from Ole Blue, held it up by its two hind legs, and looked it over. "I'll skin it when we get home," he said. "Then Ma can fry it up for dinner."

Jeannie sighed and looked away. She felt sorry about the whole thing. Then she remembered what Pa always said, when he saw the sad look on her face, after some animal had been killed for food. He'd give her braid a little yank and say, "Punkin, God put some critters here on this earth for us to eat. And--that's the way it is."

Jeannie and Henry trudged along in silence. For a time, Jeannie thought about Mrs. Lengenfeld and her daughter. "Helga's awful shy," she said. "Hardly spoke a word."

"She's just new to Texas," Henry said.

"Well, she sure seems nice."

Jeannie climbed the back porch steps. She was already making plans for her next visit with Helga. "And, you know, Henry, I think, we're going to be good friends," she said, entering the house.

Chapter 8
"Facing Danger with Diamond"

The next day, Ma lifted a dried, pork sausage from the deep, lard bucket in the kitchen pantry. "I think Mrs. Lengenfeld will want this sausage," she said, packing it in a small basket.

Jeannie remembered their hog butchering activities last fall. They'd hung the sausage links in rows on the smokehouse rafters. Later, when the cured sausage was ready to eat, Ma had put some in the pantry lard bucket for their immediate use.

"Yes'm," Jeannie said. "I think she'll like it, too. I love to eat butter bread and sausage sandwiches."

Ma smiled and said, "I know you do, dear."

When Ma gave Mrs. Lengenfeld the sausage, Jeannie watched a bright smile circle Mrs. Lengenfeld's round face. "Oh, tank you, tank you, Ruth," she said, hugging Ma. "Gott bless you. Ve had no sausage since ve left Kassel, Germany."

"And thank you for that delicious coffeecake, Emma," Ma said, returning the hug. "We enjoyed every bite of it."

The ladies entered the Markham parlor. Ma found her knitting in her basket, and Mrs. Lengenfeld continued crocheting a tablecloth, while they chatted together like old friends.

In the kitchen, Jeannie pointed to the black stove and said, "Stove, Helga."

Helga nodded and smiled. "Stove," she said.

"Table," Jeannie said, touching the tabletop.

Helga repeated the word quickly.

"Chair," Jeannie said.

"Chair," Helga echoed.

Jeannie lifted a spoon from a flatware jar on the table and said, "Spoon."

Outdoors, Jeannie gave Helga the English words for objects in the yard. Helga told Jeannie the German words.

Soon Jeannie giggled and said, "Helga, you learn English better than I learn German. I can't roll my 'R's' like you do." It was too much like the whistle, she couldn't learn, when Henry tried to teach her. "Sorry, Helga," Jeannie said, shaking her head. "That 'R' rolling sound is really hard for me."

Jeannie visited Helga often in the following days. Since a barbed wire fence separated their ranches, instead of walking through the pasture today, Jeannie decided to ride Diamond on the dirt road leading to the Markham ranch. And Ole Blue tagged along happily.

"He is so big, so tall!" Helga exclaimed, when Jeannie arrived on Diamond.

As Jeannie dismounted, there was fear in Helga's voice, "He might bite me,"she said.

"Go get a sugar cube from your Ma," Jeannie said softly.

When her friend returned, Jeannie brought Diamond's face closer to Helga's outstretched palm. "Ohh!" Helga squealed, while Diamond's lips gently scooped the sugar lump from her hand.

Jeannie gave Helga, Diamond's halter reins. "Lead him around the yard," she said.

"Do you tink I can do it?" Helga asked, hesitantly.

"Sure you can," Jeannie said. "Diamond likes you."

Slowly, Helga led him around in a circle. After a time, she patted his forehead and then his neck.

Jeannie took the reins and led Diamond to the

porch, where she easily mounted him. "Come on up here, and I'll give you a little ride," she invited, with a coaxing smile.

Swallowing her fear, Helga climbed up on Diamond's rump. She sat behind Jeannie and wrapped her arms tightly around her friend's waist.

"Now, Helga, let's go for a little gallop," Jeannie said. "Diamond has a nice gait. You'll like it. Just hold on tight."

"Okay," Helga whispered, "but don't go too fast."

Jeannie tapped Diamond's sides gently with her boot heels. He found a slow gait that was just the right tempo. Ole Blue and Lady scampered after the girls.

"I think Diamond knows you're a little scared," Jeannie said. "He's not going very fast."

Helga giggled, "Vell, I tink ve are flying!" she shouted happily.

"Yes," Jeannie said, with a chuckle. "By grannies! Ve are flying!" She brought Diamond to a walk and turned back toward the ranch house. Ole Blue and Lady dashed away, playing a game of chase.

"Don't play rough, Blue!" Jeannie called.

"Dos two dogs are good friends," Helga said.

Jeannie chuckled. "Ole Blue likes to run and romp around with Lady, but sometimes, he plays a little too rough with her. I have to always warn him about that."

Mr. Markham watched from the porch steps as the girls rode up. "Howdy, Jeannie," he said, tipping his wide-brimmed hat.

"Howdy, Mr. Markham," Jeannie said.

"Looks like you've done gone and taught Helga not to be afraid to ride a horse."

"Reckon so," Jeannie said, with a satisfied grin.

"Helga, I have a gentle mare in the barn," Mr. Markham said. "Her name's Susie. You could ride her. Then you and Jeannie could go riding together."

"Oh, Mr. Markham, what vould Mutter say?" Helga asked, anxiously biting her lower lip.

"I've already talked to her about it," Mr. Markham said, twisting his long, gray mustache. "It's fine with her, if you want to ride Susie."

"But I don't know how to ride all by myself," Helga said, hesitantly.

"I'll teach you," Jeannie said quickly. "I'll show you how to saddle up and how to ride."

"Well, Helga," Mr. Markham said, "Do you want Jeannie to teach you?"

"Oh ja, sure," Helga said, growing flustered. "I just hope I learn."

"You will," Jeannie said confidently. "It'll be as easy as falling off a log."

Mr. Markham smiled. "Then, that settles it," he said. "Let's go to the barn and saddle Miss Susie."

Later that evening, when Jeannie and Ma were cleaning the supper dishes, Jeannie said, "You know, Ma, once Helga got some confidence and lost her fear, she took to riding a horse, like a duck takes to water."

"I'm glad you have a new friend living close by," Ma said. She put a clean mixing bowl in the cabinet.

"And now, we both have a horse," Jeannie said, hanging the dishtowel on a hook beside the sink. "And we can ride together and talk and have fun; and ole Blue and Lady can run along with us and have fun, too."

"Just be careful, dear," Ma cautioned. "You're used

to ranch life, but Helga isn't. Don't let her get hurt."

"I won't, Ma," Jeannie said.

Often when the girls went riding together, Diamond slowed his pace for Susie; but today, as the girls rode the trail west to the Leon River, he tugged at the reins, forcing Jeannie to let him run as fast as he could.

Glancing back, Jeannie glimpsed Susie following in an easy, loping gait. She had to give the little mare credit. Susie wasn't trying to keep up with Diamond. Susie was smart enough to know she couldn't do it. And Lady wasn't about to run herself ragged either! She and Ole Blue were jogging along beside Susie with their tongues hanging out and wagging their tails, just like they were swatting flies! Well, it was nice of Ole Blue to slow down for his little friend.

Jeannie reined in Diamond and let him rest while the others caught up.

"Dot Diamond can run like the wind!" Helga exclaimed, drawing close.

"He sure can," Jeannie agreed. "He's some fine horse. One night, about the time you got here from Germany, the Comanches tried to steal him."

"Really!" Helga cried. "Vot happened?"

When Jeannie finished telling Helga all about her dreadful night, she added, "So you know, for a fact, I'm really glad to have Diamond back again." Leaning over his shoulder, she stroked his neck lovingly.

Then she saw it! A diamond-back rattlesnake lay just a few feet away, near a pile of rocks, waiting, coiled, and ready. With its black, beady eyes fixed on Diamond, it shook angry, warning rattles and raised its head to strike.

Diamond pricked up his ears, snorted, and reared

backward, almost bumping into Susie. Ole Blue and Lady barked loudly!

"Stop, Helga!" Jeannie shouted. "A rattler! Oh dear Lord, please help us," she murmured.

The snake lunged at Diamond's left foreleg, but Diamond quickly sidestepped away. Jeannie continued yanking him backward.

Ole Blue pricked up his ears and growled angrily. He stiffened, ready to charge.

"No! Ole Blue, no!" Jeannie cried. "Lady, come! Let's go!"

Wheeling their horses around, the girls raced back the way they had come as both dogs followed closely behind.

"Dot was awful!" Helga said, white-faced with fear. She pulled on the reins to slow Susie down. "I vas asking Gott to help us."

"So was I," Jeannie said, reining in beside her. "Thank You, God, for saving us from that great, big rattler."

"Good ting you call the dogs back," Helga said, wide-eyed.

"Well, I, sure enough, didn't want Ole Blue or Lady to get snake bit. Sometimes, dogs die from rattlesnake bites, and, of course, so can people."

"Ve go home now," Helga said, taking a deep breath. "Dot give me such a scare."

"Right. Let's head on back. We'll go to the river tomorrow after church. I'm a little shaky myself," Jeannie admitted. "And tonight, I'll make sure Diamond gets an extra, big helping of oats!"

"Dot goes for my little Susie, too!" Helga said.

Chapter 9
"Jeannie Counts Her Blessings"

That evening, inside Diamond's stall, Jeannie gave him a hug and a final pat and said, "Enjoy your dinner." She watched him nibble oats from his feeding trough. "But don't eat too fast, young man," she cautioned. "I've given you lots of oats."

Jeannie jogged up the path to the house. It was bath night, and she was first in the tub. From the back wall of the house, Pa had already brought in the silver-colored washtub hanging there and set it on the kitchen floor.

Ma always used the tub for rinsing clothes, after she'd boiled them in the black, iron kettle in the back yard. And most nights, the family washed up in a wash basin on the back porch before going to bed, but tonight, Ma has already heated several buckets of water on the stove.

On this hot evening in late June, it was steamy in the kitchen, but Jeannie was glad to bathe first. Climbing in the tub, she thought about her adventures with that ugly rattler. Everyone knew how much she liked most critters, but she, sure enough, did despise snakes! She reached for Ma's homemade soap, determined to wash away all the day's dirt and grime.

"Oh, grannies! I'm mighty glad nothing bad happened," she told herself, scrubbing her face with soap. "I'll be counting all my blessings in Sunday School tomorrow. And, I sure do thank You, again, Lord, for saving Helga and me, and the dogs, from that mean, old rattler."

Jeannie held her right leg above the tub and rubbed it with a washcloth. It would be nice to say, "Howdy," to folks from neighboring ranches tomorrow, when they all gathered at the church down the road from Mr. Markham's ranch. Since farms and ranches were scattered far apart, Jeannie knew some folks patiently rode several hours in their buggies and wagons to get to church. She sighed and reached for her towel. She was glad her family lived near church.

Early the next morning, Jeannie slipped on her flower-patterned, gingham dress that touched her ankles. She liked her Sunday dress. It had a pretty, white lace collar and bone buttons down the front to her waist. Ma had sewn the dress by hand, and Jeannie was proud to wear it, although, if she were asked to tell the truth, she would have to say, she was more comfortable in her overalls.

Gazing in her oak dresser's mirror, Jeannie carefully plaited her long, sandy-colored hair in two, separate braids. She thought about Helga's pretty hair. It was almost pure white. And her skin was so fair. Compared to Helga, she was as brown as a gingerbread cookie.

Jeannie felt sorry for her friend. She had such delicate skin! It was during their first few days of riding their horses together, that Helga suffered painful sunburn on her face. After that, her ma made her wear a sunbonnet, and the shade it gave, helped protect her face from the sun. Well, Jeannie knew she'd never have to worry, too much, about sunburns.

She tied green, silk ribbons on her braids to match the green colors in her dress. "Can't use my cowboy boots today," she whispered. "Got to wear my black, patent-leather shoes."

She lifted her dress to her knees for a good look at her high-top shoes. "And it won't be easy to close those six, tiny buttons on the side of each ankle, either," she told herself. Sighing, she stooped over and reached for one foot, dreading the task ahead. "Whew!" she said, breathing hard, when she finished the last button. "Grannies! That was a job!"

Henry and Jeannie entered the Sunday School classroom for young people in the white-steeple church. The bigger room was for the adult Sunday School. The main Sunday services were also conducted there, later in the morning.

In the Young People's room, cane-bottomed chairs faced a small, round table covered with a lace, crocheted tablecloth. In the center lay the Holy Bible and a fruit jar of wild flowers.

"Morning, Mrs. Thompson," Jeannie said.

A petite, red-haired lady with round, black-rimmed eyeglasses smiled back. "Morning, Jeannie. Y'all come in and sit down."

"Howdy, Anna Belle," Jeannie said, speaking to a dark-haired girl in the second row.

"Howdy," Anna Belle said. She smiled, showing pretty, white teeth.

From the middle of the front row, Helga beckoned Jeannie to an empty chair beside her.

"Howdy, Mr. Jack Jenkins," Henry said, greeting his friend, whose family farmed land northeast of the Markham ranch. He gave Jack a formal handshake, in a mock show of respect, and with a pleasant grin, moved along the row to sit beside him and his younger brother. Henry nodded to Jack's brother and said, "How are you, Billy Joe?"

"Doing fine," Billy Joe said.

Jeannie leaned around Helga and nodded to a girl sitting beside her. "Howdy, Linda Mae,"she said.

Linda Mae smiled hello. Jeannie knew Linda Mae Johnson was about Henry's age. It was no secret to Jeannie that Henry and Linda Mae were special friends. She knew they always spoke to one another after church. Linda Mae would often giggle, and look up and smile at Henry. Sometimes Henry's face would turn a little red, and he would shift from one foot to the other.

Jeannie smiled and nodded to a couple of other kids in the row behind her, but now, it was time to begin.

Mrs. Thompson opened her Bible. "I'm reading from Psalm 23," she said softly.

"The Lord is my shepherd, I shall not want. He maketh me to lie down in green pastures..."

The half-opened window behind Mrs. Thompson was propped up with a piece of cedar word against its inside frame. Sunlight, streaming through the narrow windowpane, crossed in front of the small table.

Jeannie sighed in deep contentment. She felt a wonderful peace inside. Everything about the simply, furnished room gave off a tranquil holiness. She studied the wall painting behind Mrs. Thompson. It was a picture of a fat baby Jesus, held in the arms of a Madonna. Mrs. Thompson had once said that it was a copy of a painting by an Italian artist from the 1600's.

Outside the window, Jeannie noticed bright, yellow sunflowers growing in tall clusters in the grassy churchyard. On beyond were Mr. Markham's cotton fields, already blooming and turning white in the June sun.

The thin, lacy curtains fluttered, as a gentle breeze carried with it, the scent of rich soil and growing things.

Jeannie breathed in deeply. How easy it was to love God and His beautiful world today!

After Sunday School, the young people joined their parents in the church sanctuary. From a large, cowhide armchair, facing the congregation, a tall, slim, middle-aged man wearing a somber, black suit, rose and stood behind the pulpit. His face was lined, and his thick, black hair was graying at the temples.

Reverend Thompson's hawk-like eyes swept over the sanctuary. He looked into the face of each worshiper. Then his deep voice rang out, "Folks, I'd like for y'all to please turn in your hymn books to page three hundred and nineteen. Now, please stand and join with me in singing, 'What a Friend We Have in Jesus'."

Jeannie glanced at Mrs. Thompson, sitting on a round stool, near the pulpit. Her yellow-flowered, organdy dress spread around her legs like a pretty fan, as she turned and pressed her feet up and down on the pump organ's pedals in the opening chords of the hymn.

Pastor Thompson led the singing in a clear, baritone voice. Jeannie knew the song, but Helga held a hymnal to learn the English words.

When the hymn ended, Pastor Thompson asked the congregation to bow their heads in prayer. "Our Heavenly Father," he said, with closed eyes, "we are gathered here today to sing praises to Thy name and to worship Thee. Help us, oh God, to do Thy will, and to ask forgiveness for our sins; for sinners, we all are. Make our fields fruitful and our crops bountiful. And give us the strength and good health to do Thy will. Bless us and make us pure in heart. We ask all this in the precious name of Thy son, Jesus. Amen."

"Amen," echoed several male voices, including Pa's.

"Amen," Jeannie whispered. "And, dear Lord, thank You, again, for keeping Helga and me, and the horses and dogs, safe from that old rattler--oh, yes, I almost forgot; please help me to be willing to pick cotton, when the time comes." Jeannie remembered, Pa had talked about that dreadful task, just this morning!

"Looks like we'll be picking cotton come early August," Pa had said. "Weather's been so warm. It's getting ripe pretty fast. Guess your play-time is just about over, Punkin." Then he had given Jeannie's shoulder a sympathetic pat, because he knew she, sure enough, hated picking cotton.

Well, there was one bright spot. She and Helga had a few more weeks together, and today, they could spend the afternoon at the river and go wading in the shallow water along the riverbanks.

Chapter 10
"Helga's Secret"

Nearing the river in the late afternoon, the girls glimpsed the tall oak trees with their limbs hanging over its banks. "Looks shady and cool," Jeannie said.

"I hope so," Helga said. "I vant to take off my shoes and go vade in the water."

"Me, too," Jeannie said. "Let's ride faster." With a kick of her heels, she prodded Diamond into a trot. Susie kept up with him, but both girls suffered, in their rumps, from the bumpy gait.

They trotted past summer grass and thick weeds growing along the riverbank and finally stopped in a clearing among the shady trees.

"Look, Helga," Jeannie said, dismounting. She pointed to a few trees nestled among the oaks. "They're loaded with ripe pecans."

"Ja," Helga said, "dey look big!"

After Helga dismounted, Jeannie noticed the affectionate way their horses nuzzled one another, but she didn't mention it.

Helga began pulling brown pecans from a heavy, tree branch. She laughed and exclaimed, "They are falling right in my hands."

"That's because they're ready to eat," Jeannie explained.

The girls, each, found two stones for themselves. Placing a nut on one stone and using the other for a hammer, they tapped their nut, cracking its shell. Patiently, they picked the tiny morsels from the hull and plopped the fresh-tasting meat into their mouths.

"Umm! Dey are so goot!" Helga said, chewing and swallowing the delicious, little bites. "I never eat pecans before."

"Is that a fact!" Jeannie exclaimed. "Pecan trees grow wild all around here." She dropped another tasty tidbit in her mouth. "Ma makes the best pecan pies! They are so yummy!"

"Ja, let's take some pecans home with us today. I vant Mutter to taste one."

"Okay," Jeannie said, going for her lunch bucket, hanging on the saddle, on Diamond's back. "I'll get your bucket for you," she called. "But, don't eat too many of them. They're very rich. You might get a stomachache."

While filling her bucket with pecans, Jeannie noticed the horses continuing to nuzzle one another. She had not tethered them. Instead, she had left them to graze nearby. "Look, Helga," she said. "Diamond is sure acting like he's sweet on Susie. I think he's trying to mate."

Helga's face turned red. "Ja?" Helga giggled. "Maybe ve get a baby cold, sometime."

"Could be," Jeannie said, laughing. "Could be we get a baby COLT--a baby colt. Look, he's chasing Susie and trying to catch her." Jeannie was familiar with animals playing a mating game, but Helga seemed embarrassed. "Let's go to the river," Jeannie said.

The girls moved closer to the riverbank and watched the slow-moving water.

"It looks shallow," Jeannie said. "That's because we haven't had a big rain yet. I guess, we could cool off our feet."

"Oh, look, I see little pebbles in the bottom," Helga said.

"Take off your shoes," Jeannie said. "Let's go wading. We're both wearing old overalls, so we don't have to worry about getting them wet."

"It's not too deep is it?" Helga asked, timidly chewing on her lower lip.

"We'll stay close to the riverbank," Jeannie said. "Don't go out in the middle. That's where it's deep."

When the girls stepped into the slow-moving current, the water swirled around their feet and tickled their toes. Helga giggled. She lifted one foot, and then the other from the water, and held onto Jeannie's arm. "Ohhh! It's a little bit cold," she squealed.

"Not much," Jeannie said. "You'll get used to it."

They moved forward until water touched their knees. Then they stood still, enjoying its coolness. Jeannie pointed to the gnarled limb of an oak tree. "Let's wade over yonder to that tree limb hanging over the water," she said. "We can sit on it and hang our legs down in the water."

The girls waded in the knee-deep water to the tree's limb. It wiggled and swayed under their weight, but they managed to seat themselves by holding onto smaller branches. Then they let their legs dangle down in the water.

Jeannie peered into its clear depths. Bits of light sparkled on the water. "There's catfish a plenty in the river," she said.

"Catfish? I never see von yet," Helga said.

"Well, they have long whiskers like a cat, and a great, big face," Jeannie explained. "They're mighty good eating! Sometimes Pa and Henry and me come fishing in the river. Ma fries up the catfish with potatoes, and they taste so good."

Jeannie's stomach began to growl at the thought of

a tasty catfish. "Want to come with us next time we go fishing?"

"Ja, sure," Helga said.

"But--you have to learn how to bait a hook," Jeannie warned. "And, sometimes, you have to touch a live, wiggley worm, to do it."

"Ohh!" Helga squirmed in disgust. She released the branch she was holding and fell face down into the water.

The current began to push her forward. With her arms flailing in all directions, she tried to stand. "Jeannie! Help me! I don't svim!" she cried, falling backward.

Jeannie jumped in the water and swam with the current. It was taking Helga downstream toward the middle of the river.

"Dear Lord, please help me," Jeannie prayed as she swam. "Don't let Helga drown." She reached for her friend, grabbed her arm, and tugged her back toward shore, dragging her against the current.

"Keep your head up--out of the water!" Jeannie yelled.

Helga's pale-blue eyes were panic-stricken.

"Kick your feet!" Jeannie ordered, pulling Helga backward.

Helga gave a few frightened kicks. "You can touch bottom now," Jeannie said, still holding Helga's arm.

Choking and sputtering, as her feet finally touched the river bottom, Helga gasped for breath and pushed her wet hair from her eyes.

"Are you all right? Can you breathe?" Jeannie asked anxiously.

Helga nodded, coughing, and spitting out water.

Dripping wet, with their overalls clinging heavily

to their bodies, the girls struggled up the riverbank, and sprawled in exhaustion on the grass near their horses.

Diamond and Susie gave them mildly, curious glances, while they continued to chomp on the sweet, river grass.

"I vas so scared," Helga sobbed, when she had caught her breath. Tears rolled down her cheeks. "I vas praying so hard to the Lord to help me," she wailed.

"I know, Helga," Jeannie said, cradling Helga's damp head in the crook of her arms. "I asked God to help us, too, and He did. You're safe now."

As soon as Helga quieted down, Jeannie said, "Why didn't you tell me you didn't know how to swim?"

"I vas so ashamed. I kept it a secret," Helga said softly. "Jeannie, you can do so many tings. I vant to be like you!"

"Oh, grannies! Helga," Jeannie said with a chuckle. She hugged her friend close. "I'll teach you how to swim. I know a better place. There's a shallow pool in the bend of the river where it narrows down. It's safe there."

"Ja, maybe, someday," Helga said. "I only vant to go home, now."

There was just enough sun left to dry the girls' clothes, as they rode slowly back home.

"I don't tink I tell Mutter, vot happened," Helga said, chewing nervously on her lower lip. "I tink she be too vorried. I tank Gott He vas there to help us again. First, the rattlesnake yesterday, and now, the river, today. Sometimes, I tink Vest Texas is a dangerous place."

Jeannie nodded thoughtfully. "I guess you're right," she said with a sigh. "I hadn't thought much about it. Course, I was born here, so, I reckon, I'm used to ranch life," she said with a faraway look on her face. "But, I know for a fact, we have to be alert and careful all the time, since most anything can happen." Then she turned to Helga and said, "And one good thing, I know the good Lord is always watching over us. He's helped me out of many a scrape through the years."

Helga sighed and shook her head, "Vell," she said, "I can honestly say, I never had so many scares in Germany."

"I'm sure that's true, Helga," Jeannie said sympathetically. "I wish I could make ranch life easier for you. One thing I can do, is teach you how to swim, and, the sooner--the better."

Chapter 11
"Cotton, the Enemy!"

With a heavy heart, Jeannie glanced at the almanac calendar, hanging beside her oak dresser. Already, it was the second day of August. Helga and she hadn't done half the things they'd planned to do, and now, there was a bright sun rising in the east. From the way it looked, it promised to bring a hot, humid day, too!

Jeannie couldn't enjoy her breakfast. She was thinking about the cotton fields and hard work ahead. Much too early that morning, she found herself standing by the cotton weigh-in wagon.

"Look, Jeannie," Pa said cheerfully, "your sack is a lot smaller than Henry's."

Jeannie knew Pa was trying to make her feel better. But his kind words didn't erase her frown.

Pa gave her a long, gray, burlap bag with a wide, shoulder band. "It's all right, Punkin, if you can only drag twenty or thirty pounds today." Then Pa turned to Henry, waiting beside Jeannie, and said, "But, son, I want you to try and fill your sack up to a hundred."

"I'll do it, Pa," Henry said confidently. He put his arm through the strap attached to his cotton sack, hung it over his right shoulder, and settled his wide-brimmed, straw hat down, over his curly, black hair.

Jeannie stared at her enemy, those dreaded rows of brown stalks ahead, spilling over with long, fluffy, white bolls of cotton. "I'll do the best I can, Pa," she said, taking a deep breath.

Dressed in overalls, and one of Henry's blue, long-sleeved, cotton shirts, Jeannie remembered Ma telling her, "The long sleeves keep the hot sun off your arms--keeps them from blistering. And wear this sunbonnet, too. You'll need it."

Jeannie tied the bonnet under her chin. She put on a pair of white, cotton gloves to protect her fingers from the sharp pricks of dried bolls, unwilling to give up cotton.

Then, under Henry's approving eyes, she pulled kneepads over her knees and hung the cotton sack across her chest and right shoulder.

"We'll just take one row and not try to pick two rows at a time," Henry said. "Let's make a game, and see who gets down to the end of his row first, Shorty."

"You will. I don't doubt that for a second," Jeannie said. Her voice lacked enthusiasm as she went on, "But, if you want me to, I'll race you."

Her sunbonnet provided a sunshade, while she stared ahead, trying to see the end of her cotton row. "Think I'll just bend over and pick for awhile," she decided.

"When your back give out, you'll kneel mighty quick," Henry said, but he also chose to bend over his row. Looking across to Jeannie he chanted, "All right, now--on your mark, get set, go!"

In a strong burst of energy, Jeannie's fingers grasped a cotton boll. Dropping the white ball of cotton into the limp, wide-mouthed sack under her arm, she carefully gleaned the plant. Pa had said earlier, to pick each boll on the plant, as clean and free of cotton, as she could. When she reached the end of the row, she straightened. Her back felt a little stiff, but it might be fun if she could really keep up with Henry. He had just finished his row.

Switching to another row, Jeannie said, "Okay, you won the first row. I'm ready for the second row. Let's go!"

About halfway down the row, Jeannie's sack was growing heavier. She pushed the cotton deeper and packed it solid to make more room for a full bag. Already, she could feel the sun's heat, on the back of her neck, burning through her sunbonnet. She rubbed her tongue across her upper lip and tasted salt.

"It's no use," she told herself, "I have to give up." She called to Henry a few feet ahead, "You win!" Sinking down on her kneepads, she leaned back on her heels and rested.

"Ah-hah!" Henry said. "Giving out, are you, Shorty?"

In spite of his joking words, Jeannie noticed the tired look of relief on her brother's face, when he knelt to rest beside a cotton plant. She rubbed her sleeve across her forehead and loosened the sunbonnet ties. It helped a little, yet her mouth felt as dry as the cotton she was picking. She couldn't wait to get back to the burlap-covered canteen, hanging in the shade, under the wagon bed. "I'm as thirsty as a dying man in the Sahara Desert in Africa!" she murmured to herself.

"Hey, Shorty," Henry said, swinging his arm in a circular motion, "look at how much is left." Row upon row stretched out before them--like a white, cotton blanket.

Henry sighed and shook his head "Can't pick it all today," he said, wearily.

"Oh, grannies! It's a lot, and my back is already good and tired!" Jeannie murmured, sinking down on her sack. She hugged her knees to her chin, and watched a line of giant, red ants march slowly around her boot, over tiny, dirt clods, to a high mound, under a dried-up cotton plant. A fat, green grasshopper darted by. Overhead, the hot sun continued its blazing course across the cloudless sky toward noon. In the distance, a black crow called to his companion--another black crow, sitting on a fence post at the field's edge.

Jeannie rose. "Well, we might as well go on," she said resolutely. She adjusted her shoulder strap, knelt, and reached for a full cotton boll.

At last, Pa called a halt for dinner. He weighed and emptied his cotton sack; then Ma's, and Henry's next, and finally, Jeannie's sack. "You pulled fifty-five pounds of cotton. That's mighty good!" Pa said smiling. "Reckon, you pulled about half your weight, Punkin."

Jeannie was too hot to fully appreciate Pa's compliment. She had just enough strength left to crawl wearily to the shade, underneath the wagon, where Ole Blue had been lying all morning.

"Howdy, Blue," she murmured, patting his sleepy head. "You're a mighty smart, hound dog. You don't have any intention of getting out there in that hot sun today, do you old feller?"

Ole Blue thumped his tail and yawned. Jeannie opened the canteen and let the cool water flow down her parched throat. Groaning, she slipped off her sweaty gloves and bonnet, spread out on her empty cotton sack, and lay down next to Ole Blue.

"Whoo-EE! My whole body's aching!" she moaned, scratching behind Blue's ears. "How am I going to make it through the sultry afternoon?"

Ole Blue licked her hand. "You're listening to me whimper and carry on, feeling sorry for myself, aren't you," Jeannie said. "But you have to admit, it's a nasty job. I'm all sweaty and gritty with dirt." She closed her eyes and lay there, dreaming of a cool swim in the Leon River.

"Hungry, Shorty?" Henry asked, stooping under the wagon wheel, holding a tin, molasses bucket in his hand.

Jeannie hadn't been thinking about food. Besides, it was too hot to eat anyway.

Henry plopped down beside her and sat cross-legged. He lifted a few wedges of cucumber pickles, and some deviled egg sandwiches from the bucket, and offered Jeannie a sandwich.

At first, she bit into the sandwich half-heartedly. Then her mouth began to water. "Reckon I'm hungry, after all," she said, with her mouth stuffed full of food. She sat upright and wolfed down the entire sandwich, and then another.

All too soon, Pa poked his head under the wagon. "Y'all ready to pick some more cotton?" he asked.

"I reckon so," Jeannie replied, with little enthusiasm.

Pa winked. "Aw, it'll give you muscles, Punkin," he said, walking away.

"Don't think I want any," Jeannie whispered. Then, she felt a twinge of shame. "Got to take the good with the bad on the farm!" she scolded herself. "When some hard work comes along, you carry on like a spoilt, little crybaby!"

With a deep sigh, Jeannie shouldered her empty cotton sack and struck off with Henry, past the already gleaned, dried, brown stalks--on to the rows of white, cotton bolls, still waiting, heavy and full.

Chapter 12
"School Days Bring Mischief and Problems"

"Will cotton-picking time ever end?" Jeannie wondered, as two, long, tiring weeks dragged by. Each day she rose early to help with the chores. After chores were finished, the family trudged to the cotton fields. They returned at sundown with aching muscles.

To Jeannie, the best part of the workday, was early evening. Then, in the twilight, wearing dusty, work clothes, everyone climbed inside the round, water tank. Most of the year it was used for watering stock. However, during cotton-picking time, after each day in the fields, everyone took a good wash in the tank.

By the first week of September, all the cotton was picked. Jeannie felt like jumping for joy! At last! No more picking cotton for a whole year. School was beginning on Monday--only two days away! She could hardly wait.

When Monday morning finally arrived, Jeannie pulled on her clean overalls and her boots. It didn't matter that she wasn't wearing a dress to school. She only had one dress, anyway--it was her Sunday church dress.

Since school was in the church building, it wasn't too far away, but today, Jeannie saddled up Diamond and rode to school. She knew he'd have to stand tethered in the churchyard, which was now the schoolyard, during the week. So, she wasn't planning to ride him to school every day, because he needed to be running free in the pasture at home.

"It's not fair to keep him penned up, every day," Pa said.

Jeannie agreed with Pa. Most days she would walk to school.

Today Pastor Thompson "wore a different hat"--

like Pa said--because he became a teacher for the older kids, and Mrs. Thompson taught the younger children in the smaller, Sunday School room.

Jeannie and the other students sat in cane-bottomed chairs. Several tables of various sizes were used as desks. Two students sat at a table. Most students were at different grade levels, but they shared books and materials whenever possible.

Just as Jeannie had hoped, Helga and she sat at the same table and worked from the same books. In most subjects, Jeannie was a good student, but when it came to arithmetic, she had to admit, Helga was a whiz!

"No, Jeannie," Helga whispered one day, noticing that Jeannie had solved a math problem incorrectly on her slate. "Erase dot answer. Vatch me," she said. "Dis is the vay you do it." Then, Helga showed Jeannie how to divide mixed fractions and get the correct answers.

The girls weren't worried about their whispers. Since Pastor Thompson couldn't go to each person immediately when they needed help, the students were allowed to help one another, as long as they did it quietly and only discussed their lessons.

Walking to school one, cool, autumn morning in October, Jeannie noticed the landscape was graying, and all the fields were plain, brown soil lying at rest. Nothing was green any more. She felt a twinge of melancholy. Even most of the birds and little creatures seemed to have disappeared.

Later on in class, she felt better, because she had begun to read a book called THE ADVENTURES OF TOM SAWYER, a new story for young people, written by a Mississippi River boat captain, by the name of Mark

Twain.

There was something special about the way Mark Twain could tell a story. Jeannie found herself enjoying the book and thinking how much she liked Tom Sawyer. He was her kind of friend. Seems like he was always up to some kind of mischief, and he was always getting into trouble. She liked Becky, his girlfriend, too. She was sweet and wasn't afraid to join in with Tom on his adventures.

Just as Jeannie was reaching the good part, where Tom and Becky were lost in the cave, and their candles were burning low, she felt a nudge from Helga. Her friend was passing a note to her.

With a furtive glance around, Jeannie took the note. She knew Pastor Thompson was very firm about kids not writing notes to one another. He expected them to pay attention, at all times, to their schoolwork. But she took the note, put it in her copy of Tom Sawyer, unfolded it, and read:

"Billy Joe is pulling my hair when Pastor Thompson turns his back. I hate Billy Joe!"

Jeannie frowned and folded the note. She turned and glared at Billy Joe sitting at the table behind Helga. A sly smile was on his face. Jeannie doubled up her fist and shook it at him.

Billy Joe wrinkled up his nose. Then, when Jeannie stuck her tongue out at Billy Joe, Pastor Thompson saw her do it. He stood beside her table.

"Well, Miss Hanson," he said, in a deep, stern voice, "it seems you don't have anything to do, but stick your tongue out at other classmates. I think you will stay after school today and help me clean the room."

Helga gave Jeannie a sympathetic glance.

Jeannie nodded obediently. Just as she turned around, the crumpled note fell to the floor. Pastor Thompson picked it up, slowly unfolded it, and read it.

"Hmm! So Miss Helga, you are writing notes, too," Pastor Thompson said. "You will stay after school and help Jeannie."

Helga's eyes filled with tears. Some of the other kids laughed at the girls' punishment, but when Pastor Thompson gave them a dark look, they put their eyes back down on their work.

Then he turned to Billy Joe. "And you, young man, you will stay after school and bring in plenty of firewood for the stove. If you need to chop more wood, you will do so. I want a good supply stored up."

From the corner of her eye, Jeannie watched Billy Joe's face turn crimson. "Good," she murmured. "It's all your fault anyway, Billy Joe."

That afternoon Jeannie erased the portable blackboard and dusted the erasers. Helga swept the classroom floor, and together, they both washed the tabletops. Billy Joe had already brought in several arm-loads of wood. They could still hear his ax hitting logs, splitting them into small, dry, kindling pieces, that later, would burn easily.

Pastor Thompson sat at his table correcting composition books. When the girls finished their work at four o'clock, they stood before him at his table.

Without glancing up, he said, "Very good girls. And remember class time is valuable. You'll be glad for all the time you spent in school when you're older."

He gave them a long stare from under his bushy

eyebrows. "Now, y'all go home before it gets too late." He glanced out the window. "The sky is growing dark. It looks like it might rain. Tell Billy Joe, I said he is also excused to go home."

Helga and Jeannie grabbed their coats and hurried outside behind the church. They watced as Billy Joe swung his ax and sent a small, flat-shaped log splintering in half.

"You got Helga and me into trouble, Billy Joe!" Jeannie scolded angrily.

"Ja, you pull my hair. Dot hurts!" Helga chimed in.

"Aw, don't be a crybaby, Helga," Billy Joe said grinning.

"Dot's not funny!" Helga replied huffily, backing away.

"I'm sorry, Helga," Billy Joe said. "Honest, I didn't mean to hurt you. I just wanted to touch your hair. It feels like white cotton, just like I thought."

"Ja, vell, you gave it a good yank, too!" Helga said indignantly. She trounced off down the road toward home.

Jeannie followed, shouting over her shoulder, "Pastor Thompson says you can quit now!"

Billy Joe soon caught up with the girls.

"Go avay! Ve're not valking mitt you!" Helga said, quickening her pace. She chewed angrily on her lower lip.

"Aw! Come on, Helga. I said, I was sorry," Billy Joe complained, matching strides with them. He hung his head and kicked at a stone in his path. "What more can I do?" he asked mournfully.

Helga slowed her pace. "All right! But don't pull my hair anymore."

The trio strolled along the road, as it sliced through

the wide, flat prairie. Except for a few withered, mesquite bushes, the prairie looked barren and desolate. A slight wind was stirring. It blew against their faces.

"The sky sure is getting dark in the east," Billy Joe observed. "We'd better high-tail it home. It could be a tornado rising way over yonder. We'd better start running."

They broke into a fast jog. Reaching a north turn in the road, Billy Joe waved goodbye, and raced toward home.

By the time the girls were in sight of the Markham ranch, the sky had darkened into a funnel-like, black cloud. "I think it's a twister coming," Jeannie said, breathing hard. "Helga, run as fast as you can. The wind is picking up."

The wind was almost a roar. Both girls burst into a swift sprint up the trail toward the ranch house. The ugly, black cloud was just a few miles away.

"I can see someone standing on the front porch," Jeannie shouted.

A man mounted a black horse at the hitching rail and sped toward the girls.

"I'm so tired, Jeannie," Helga said, almost stumbling. "My sides hurt."

"Don't stop, Helga! Keep running!" Jeannie prodded, watching the black cloud growing and drawing closer. "It's a twister for sure!"

As the rider approached, Jeannie saw it was Mr. Markham. When he pulled his stallion to a fast stop before the girls, it reared up on its hindquarters and then touched back down on the earth.

"Whoa, Blackie!" Mr. Markham commanded,

jerking on the reins. He slipped a foot from his stirrup and shouted over the roaring wind, "Get up behind me, Jeannie." He leaned down and lifted Helga to the front of his saddle. Jeannie stepped into the empty stirrup and swung up behind him.

"Haa! Blackie, run!" Mr. Markham yelled. He touched Blackie with his boot heels. Jeannie locked her arms tightly around Mr. Markham's waist and pressed her face against his heavy sheepskin jacket, as they raced to the storm cellar in back of the ranch house.

Mrs. Lengenfeld waited on the steps, arms outstretched. The wind flapped her apron. Wisps of yellow hair from her tightly, woven braids blew across her anxious face.

"Helga!" she screamed, "Come, child!"

Mr. Markham lowered Helga into Mrs. Lengenfeld's waiting arms. She carried Helga down the cellar steps, holding her close against her bosom.

"Jeannie! Inside!" Mr. Markham shouted.

Jeannie slid off Blackie's rump and scurried down the steps into the dimly lighted cellar. Mr. Markham led Blackie down the steps, while several cowhands struggled to close and lock the cellar door.

An ear-splitting roar passed over the barn. Then the loud, splintering sounds of wood crashing and flying around the yard echoed throughout the dark cellar.

Mrs. Lengenfeld turned up the lighted wick of a kerosene lamp sitting atop a flour barrel. Helga clung to her mother, sobbing quietly.

Jeannie looked at her friend. Helga was scared, but then, so was she. And all the cowhands, sitting on a bench against the wall, had worried looks on their faces. Jeannie recognized them. They had helped Pa take back his stolen horses. The tall one was Slim—the one who'd said nice things to her.

"How're you doing, little lady?" Slim asked, moving over to give her room to sit down.

"Oh, grannies!" Jeannie said nervously. "We barely made it." She twisted a strand of loose hair around her finger. "If it hadn't been for Mr. Markham and Blackie..."

"Yeah," Slim said, "Blackie's a fast horse."

"Well, boys," Mr. Markham said, stroking Blackie's face, "I got a feeling the barn is gone." He sighed heavily.

"Reckon that's so," a cowhand murmured softly.

Jeannie glanced around the silent little group huddled together in the cellar. The roar of the wind was dying down. In fact, it was so quiet outside it almost seemed like it was a hot, summer night.

"Slim, you and Waco open her up, and we'll have a look," Mr. Markham said.

Slim joined Waco at the door. Lifting the wooden bar that lay across the cellar door flaps, they pushed them apart, until the flaps lay flat on the ground, on either side of the cellar steps.

From where she sat, Jeannie could see the sky was no longer pitch-black. It had a slight, orange glow and was growing dark naturally.

"Yeah, Mr. Markham, it's a mess out here. Barn's gone." Slim shook his head in wonderment and disbelief. "Y'all can come out now," he said.

Standing with the others, at the cellar entrance, Jeannie surveyed the awful damage. Slim was right. Except for a few pieces of wood here and there, there wasn't a barn anymore.

Mr. Markham guided Blackie up the steps. "Whew!" he said with a long, low whistle. "That was some tornado!"

"Tank Gott, the house is still here," Mrs. Lengenfeld said softly.

"Yes, Emma," Mr. Markham agreed. "Thank God for that." He turned to Jeannie and said, "Missy, I want you to stay the night with Helga. It's best for right now," he added.

Jeannie's face clouded into a frown. Didn't Mr. Markham know she wanted to go home and find out if her folks were all right?

It seemed as if Mr. Markham had read her thoughts, for he turned to Slim and said, "Take Blackie. Ride over and find out how the Hanson's made out. And tell them, Jeannie's okay."

As Slim mounted, Mr. Markham stood beside him. He spoke a few words that Jeannie couldn't hear, glancing over at her, with a serious look on his face.

Slim listened to Mr. Markham's instructions. He nodded his head once or twice, then turned, and put Blackie into a fast lope down the trail.

Jeannie sighed. She supposed Mr. Markham didn't want her to go home, in case someone was hurt, or there was some kind of trouble. Well, she'd just have to wait and find out. But it wouldn't be easy.

Chapter 13
"Trouble for Diamond"

That night when the girls said their prayers kneeling at the foot of Helga's oak bed, Jeannie read the crocheted, white-lace runner attached to its wooden headboard. It said, "There is Sweet Rest in Heaven." She knew Mrs. Lengenfeld had hand-crocheted it. Above the bed was a picture of Jesus holding a little lamb in his arms.

As Helga prayed, Jeannie heard her whisper, "And tank You, Gott, for keeping us safe from the twister." Then she added, "And tank You, Gott, for keeping my friend, Jeannie, and her folks safe, too."

Helga climbed into the softness of her feather mattress and pulled the coverlet up under her chin. "See, Jeannie, I told you, Gott vould take care of your family." Helga patted Jeannie's arm reassuringly, while Jeannie settled in beside her.

"Oh, grannies, Helga! I was so glad to see Slim come riding back," Jeannie said, remembering Slim's return. "When Mr. Markham met him at the front porch, and Slim yelled, 'They're safe!' I just about busted out bawling, right then and there." She gave her pillow a hard poke. "I guess Ma and Pa and Henry were pretty scared."

Jeannie lay back with her hands clasped behind her head. "Slim said our barn lost its roof, and everything got scattered all around."

"Ja, and Mr. Markham's barn iss all gone," Helga said, with a heavy sigh. "Everyting iss a mess here, too."

In the morning Mr. Markham said, "Jeannie, climb up on Blackie behind me, and I'll take you home. I want to talk to your Pa. That tornado left us with much work to do."

On the trail, Blackie carefully skirted fallen brush

and up-rooted, little cedar trees. Debris was scattered all over the dirt road to the ranch. Nearing the house, Jeannie noticed the barn was leaning lopsided, and its roof was missing. Bits and pieces of wood were everywhere.

"Jumping grasshoppers! Just look at that mess!" Jeannie exclaimed. "And where's the haystack, Mr. Markham? I don't see it."

Mr. Markham shook his head and said, "Don't see it either. It must have blown away."

Ma and Pa stood on the porch waving to them. Henry, with his arm wrapped in a white-looking sling, joined them.

"Jeannie," Ma called, running to meet her, "are you all right?"

"I'm fine, Ma," Jeannie said, slipping off Blackie's rump and falling into Ma's outstretched arms.

"Howdy, Frank," Pa said. "Shore was some twister!"

"That's a fact, Matthew," Mr. Markham said. "How's the boy?"

"He'll be all right, won't you, son?" Pa said. "He was trying to help get the animals inside the barn before the twister hit, but the wind was so strong, it slammed him against the barn door. Gave his wrist and arm a good jolt."

"Howdy, Mr. Markham," Henry said.

Mr. Markham climbed down from Blackie and hitched him to the railing post.

"You doing all right, son?"

"Yes, sir, Mr. Markham," Henry said. "I'll be fine in a couple of days."

"Y'all come on in," Ma invited. "I've got coffee on the stove."

"All right, Ruthie, sounds good to me," Mr. Markham said.

"Outside of the barn roof, we faired, well enough," Pa said. "How'd you make out?"

"Not too bad," Mr. Markham said. "Guess, Slim told you, I lost my barn, but everything else is standing."

Pa nodded. "Shore sorry, to hear about it. Reckon, we can be thankful, we didn't lose any lives."

"That's a fact!" Mr. Markham agreed.

"Y'all come on in. You can talk in the kitchen," Ma said again, turning to go inside.

"Yes, ma'am," Mr. Markham said. "I want to talk some with Matthew about the work we got cut out for ourselves. Oh, by the way," he said, "it looks like Susie is going to have a foal in the spring. Helga says, Diamond might be the father."

Pa looked at Jeannie with a surprised expression on his face.

"He could be, Mr. Markham," Jeannie admitted. "I think Susie was in heat one day when Helga and I were riding together. Diamond was nosing her, and they were nuzzling each other. Helga and I went to pick pecans and left them for a time."

"Well, well," Pa said chuckling. He patted Mr. Markham's back. "Looks like the Markhams' and Hansons' are going to be a family!"

Mr. Markham grinned and shook Pa's hand. "Reckon that's true," he said.

"Bout that twister," Pa said, as they entered the kitchen. "It shore left us with a mess." He shook his head. "I reckon, it'll take us a month, or so, to get back on our feet and all cleaned up from that one."

"Ma, I'm going down to the barn and see Diamond," Jeannie said, watching her mother take the coffeepot from the stove and carry it to the table.

"All right, but be careful. There's a lot of brush lying around," Ma said, filling coffee cups with steaming, hot coffee.

"Don't stay long in the barn, Punkin," Pa said. "I don't know how steady it is yet. You'll find Diamond in the corral."

"All right, Pa," Jeannie said.

"Henry, you sit at the table with us. We're gonna talk about the job we got ahead of us." Pa pulled out a cane-bottomed chair. "Here, Frank, sit down," Pa invited. Then he seated himself beside Mr. Markham. Ole Blue plopped down by Henry and closed his eyes. He sighed contentedly when Henry scratched behind his long ears.

At the corral, Jeannie hugged Diamond. "I was so worried about you," she whispered, patting his face. Diamond nudged her hand. "Looking for sugar? I'm sorry, boy. I forgot to bring you some. We'll just stop up at the house, and I'll get you a lump," Jeannie promised. "Say, did you know you're going to be a daddy?"

Diamond shook his head and tossed his mane, just about the time Jeannie finished speaking. "Hmm! So you didn't know that?" Jeannie said, pretending Diamond understood her. "Well, you are, young man. You are the father of Susie's foal. I can guarantee it."

She patted his neck. "I'll get the bridle and not use a saddle today. Pa said I shouldn't stay long in the barn." Peeking inside the shadowy barn, Jeannie lifted a bridle, from the wall near the door, and left quickly.

At the house, she brought out a lump of sugar for

Diamond. He munched it while she mounted. "Ma said we can go riding around, if we're careful." Jeannie patted Diamond's mane and directed him to the north pasture.

She saw scrub oak and gray-colored sage still intact, clinging to the soil, undisturbed. Diamond worked his way through the grassy stubble of weedy growth, toward the thicket of oaks and rocky ledges beyond.

Jeannie glanced about and said, "Sure wouldn't know we had a twister go through here yesterday, Diamond. Look's like this part of the ranch wasn't bothered at all." She squinted up at the sky. "Sun's shining nice and warm--like nothing ever happened." Pa had often said the north pasture wasn't good for farming. Too many rocks and cedar trees. It was better grazing land for cattle and horses, but she liked this small section of the wilderness.

"There's a little cut-off branch of the creek that winds through Mr. Markham's place just ahead of us, Diamond," Jeannie said. "It trickles water all year round to our ranch. I expect it's full."

She leaned over and patted Diamond's neck and whispered in his ear. "Maybe, we can watch a wild deer or antelope getting a drink at the creek, if we're nice and quiet."

They paused in the shadows of several, tall cedars beside a wide, stone boulder. Jeannie slipped off Diamond's back, and cradled his face in her arms, while she gazed out at the quiet clearing near the creek.

The stillness was unbroken except for the whistle call of a bob white and the low, mournful reply of a turtledove somewhere in the distance. There was a flash of brown as a fuzzy-tailed ground squirrel scurried up the trunk of a live-oak tree. He turned to sit on a lower branch. His tiny, mouse-like face stared down at them. He wrinkled his nose and sniffed the slight breeze.

"Isn't he cute!" Jeannie whispered. She covered Diamond's nose lightly with her hand to prevent him from nickering. He flicked his ears and swished his tail.

The little, brown squirrel sat up on its haunches and rubbed its two, tiny forepaws across its cheeks.

"Howdy," Jeannie said softly. "How are you, little feller?"

Suddenly, a piercing screech tore through the stillness. Turning, Jeannie saw a huge mountain lion, leap from a rock boulder, and soar through the air, aiming for Diamond's backside.

Jeannie yanked Diamond's reins, jerking him hard. He side stepped, just as the screaming cat's sharp fangs grazed his back with a long scratch.

The huge wildcat landed on four feet, whirling as Jeannie mounted.

"Go, Diamond, go!" she shouted.

Diamond leaped forward with Jeannie clutching his reins. She hung on tightly and pressed her knees into his sides.

The angry cat pounced again, missing them, by only a few, short inches.

With Jeannie hovering over his neck, Diamond raced out of the woods into the pasture again. Glancing over her shoulder, Jeannie watched the big cat follow them for a short distance. Then it stopped and jogged back to the shadowy thicket.

Jeannie's heart was racing so hard it pounded in her ears. She slowed Diamond from his fast gallop into an easy, loping gait.

"Jumping grasshoppers! That was close," she murmured, her voice shaking. She patted Diamond's neck. "Too close!" Then she sat upright. "This is all Pa needs to hear about. After yesterday's twister, I know, he's gonna see red-hot fire, for sure!"

Jeannie burst into the kitchen as Pa and Mr. Markham were taking their last bite of Ma's blackberry, cobbler pie and finishing their coffee. "Pa! Pa!" she screeched. "There's a big, ole bobcat in the north woods. He almost got Diamond and me!"

"What's that you say, Punkin!" Pa exclaimed, scraping his chair back.

"Yes, sir, and he's a big one, too!" Jeannie added.

"I'll get my rifle. Is Diamond still outside?"

Jeannie nodded anxiously.

"I'll go with you, Matthew," Mr. Markham said, adjusting his pistol and cartridge belt.

"Let's go," Pa said, leading the way. The screened door slammed on the back porch as the men hurried outside.

Ma sighed and shook her head. "What next?" she asked. She looked Jeannie over thoroughly. "Are you all right, sugar?"

"I'm okay, Ma," Jeannie murmured. "Just scared a little."

"And I'm no help either, Shorty," Henry said, looking at his bandaged arm with disgust.

"It's all right, son," Ma consoled. "Pa and Mr. Markham will catch that ornery varmint. Sit down, Jeannie--have a cup of coffee. It will help you calm down a bit."

Jeannie was still shaking, as a picture of the big cat with its sharp, razor-like teeth, loomed up before her. "Oh, grannies, Ma! He was so big," Jeannie said, twisting her hair. "He really scared me."

Ma hugged Jeannie close and kissed her forehead. "I'm sorry, dear," she said. "All this bad weather, the noise, and the excitement must have flushed the big cat out of its lair. That's probably why it had the courage to attack you."

"Well, I'm mighty glad Diamond is a fast racer!" Jeannie said proudly.

"He's a wonderful horse, dear," Ma agreed, pouring half coffee and half milk in Jeannie's cup. "I just thank the Lord, He was there to protect you."

Soon Jeannie and Henry watched from the back yard, as Pa and Mr. Markham returned. "Yes, sir," Jeannie said, "they've got that dead bobcat sprawled across Diamond's back. He's lying in front of Pa."

"He's a big one, all right, Shorty," Henry said. "Good thing you were riding Diamond. He got you out of there in a hurry."

"Unhuh, he sure did," Jeannie said, as the men draw close.

"I helped corner him, Jeannie," Mr. Markham said, dismounting, "but your Pa here, shot him right between the eyes, dead center!"

Jeannie smiled her satisfaction. "Mr. Markham," she said, "I can't say, I'm much sorry, for that ornery, old bobcat. It was out to get Diamond and me!"

"I'm mighty glad he didn't, Punkin," Pa said, giving her a hug. "I think we'll just skin this ole feller and throw him down on the floor. He'll make a nice rug."

"Well, sir, that suits me, just fine," Jeannie said, feeling no sympathy for the wildcat that had tried to kill both Diamond and herself!

Chapter 14
"A Surprise Gift"

The next several months, folks on neighboring ranches helped one another clean up and repair damages done to everyone's property and belongings. In time, the effects of the twister were set aside as part of life on the West Texas plains.

When Jeannie asked Pa, how folks managed to accept such things so easily, without too much complaining, he said, "A twister is one of those things folks expect to happen. They do the best they can, and just hope, they'll be ready when the next one comes along."

The ranch was back in shape for Christmas festivities. It was a happy time with plenty of good food. Ma made two, chocolate layer cakes, a pecan pie, a blackberry cobbler, and a peach cobbler. She also baked a big turkey hen with lots of dressing.

As Jeannie helped in the kitchen, she said, "Ma, do you think I'll ever be as good a cook as you are?"

Ma smiled and said, "If you'd spend more time in the kitchen with me, and not so much time outdoors, you could become a good cook."

Jeannie nodded. Ma was right. That's what she'd have to do--but, maybe, when she was just a little older.

On Sunday morning, Jeannie looked out her bedroom window and saw snow on the ground. Although it wasn't much snow, she was pleased. Most of the time, the West Texas weather was just ornery and cold!

After breakfast Jeannie said, "Henry, before we get ready to go to church, let's make us a snowman."

"Sure, Shorty," Henry said. "My arm's in good shape now."

Soon, they fashioned a big snowman. They put one

of Pa's straw work hats on him and stuck a pipe in his mouth.

Pa and Ma watched the shaping of the snowman from the porch. When they saw the finished snowman, Pa laughed and shook his head.

"Why, he looks just like you, Pa," Ma said, with a teasing smile.

"Is that what you say, Missy?" Pa reached over and gave Ma a little swat on her behind. She turned and scurried back in the house, with Pa following close on her heels.

Jeannie heard her giggling when Pa caught her. Knowing Pa, and how much he loved Ma, she guessed he probably gave her a big kiss, instead of another swat.

After a beautiful, church service, with the singing of many Christmas carols, which included Jeannie's favorite carol, "Silent Night," the family returned home for a delicious Christmas dinner.

It was a wonderful feast day. Everyone ate and ate. As a special treat, Pa had brought home fresh oranges from Sam Wasserman's store.

"Seems like a train now passes through the town of Eastland about twenty miles away," Pa said, sharing the latest news he'd heard in the trading post. "Sam Wasserman's hired help drove his wagon to Eastland to pick up supplies for his store, and they brought back several feed sacks of oranges."

Later, holding her gift for Helga in her free hand, Jeannie rode Diamond to Mr. Markham's ranch.

"Oh, Jeannie," Helga squealed, looking inside the tissue of the small box. "Violet toilet water!" She squeezed the atomizer spray about her neck and arms.

"Whew!" Jeannie said, almost choking. "That's enough! You'll smell up the whole room!" Actually, the scent was too sweet to her liking, but Helga loved it.

Helga went to her dresser and brought back a small package. "Open it," she said.

"It feels heavy," Jeannie said.

"Ja," Helga said, waiting.

Jeannie uncovered a book. "Oh, Helga," she cried happily. "Where did you ever get this book?"

"I order it--from a catalog," she said smiling.

Jeannie read the title on the leather bound cover. "THE COMPLETE WORKS OF EDGAR ALLEN POE," she murmured. Then she turned happily to her friend. "You heard me say I love his mystery stories, didn't you, Helga?" she teased accusingly.

Helga nodded as Jeannie hugged her and said, "I'm so proud of the book. Thank you."

"And I love my toilet water," Helga whispered, squeezing Jeannie back. "Thank you, too! Come, Mutter has some sugar doughnuts waiting for us."

Chapter 15
"School Celebrations and a Special Valentine"

At school, all during the month of January, the students practiced activities for a combined Valentine's Day and Presidents' Day event. As a class exercise, and for practical purposes also, all twenty students wrote their parents notes, inviting them to attend class presentations to be held on Valentine's Day, February 14, 1885.

The schoolroom was changed back into a church auditorium. Chairs faced a slightly, elevated riser stretching across the front of the room.

First, the little ones recited Mother Goose Rhymes in a group chorus. Then, they sang "Mary had a Little Lamb."

After the applause ended, Pastor Thompson stood at the side podium and announced, "Miss Helga Marie Lengenfeld will sing 'Beautiful Dreamer,' by Stephen Foster. Mrs. Thompson will accompany her on the piano."

Seated with the other students in the front row, Helga glanced nervously at Jeannie beside her. Then, breathing in a deep breath, and with cheeks flaming red, she mounted the riser and waited for the piano's introductory notes to end. Softly, in clear, bell-like tones, she sang the lyrics of the plaintive melody.

Helga's sweet voice captured everyone's attention. Jeannie was especially charmed. Helga looked so pretty standing there with her long, taffy-colored hair hanging down her back. Her eyes were a beautiful blue, and her skin was so fair! She looked like a spring flower in her pale-green dress trimmed with yellow ribbons, her ma had made for the occasion.

Jeannie joined in the enthusiastic applause, as a beaming Helga returned to sit beside her. "You were wonderful," Jeannie whispered, squeezing Helga's hand. "Everyone loved your song!"

Helga smiled and nodded happily.

Earlier in January, when it had been his turn to decide what he was going to do for his presentation, Billy Joe had told everyone that his Pa was teaching him to play the banjo. It was no surprise to Jeannie, when Pastor Thompson gave an introduction, and Billy Joe played "Oh Susannah," on his banjo, to the happy, rhythmic hand clapping of the audience.

Jeannie saw that all through the piece, Billy Joe didn't seem at all nervous. In fact, he was enjoying himself so much, she suspected he would have played another tune, if he'd been asked to, but the program went on. It was close to dinnertime, and folks were probably getting hungry.

Other students recited poems or sang songs. A seventh grader named Ezra gave a talk on how to load a rifle and stalk a deer. Jeannie noticed all the men folks applauded loudly afterward.

Anna Belle who had been taking piano lessons with Mrs. Thompson played a waltz by Johann Strauss. Then it dawned on Jeannie. She was next!

"I'm not afraid," she told herself. "So, why is my heart pounding? Why is my stomach tightening up? And, grannies! Do stop twisting your hair!"

Pastor Thompson began his introduction, "Miss Jeannie Ruth Hanson will now recite 'The Gettysburg Address' in memory of our martyred President, Abraham Lincoln, a man of the people. He will long be remembered by all Americans."

Jeannie stepped up on the riser and looked out at

Ma's smiling face. Pa gave her a coaxing nod and a wink. Even Henry looked away from her. Jeannie knew he didn't want to make a face and cause her to laugh.

"Four score and seven years ago..." Jeannie stared out at the sea of faces in the room-- "our fathers brought forth on this continent a new nation, conceived in liberty and dedicated to the proposition that all men are created equal."

Suddenly her heart soared, as she considered those important words, scribbled hurriedly on the back of an envelope, while President Lincoln was traveling by train to dedicate the Gettysburg Battlefield as a National Cemetery.

She spoke slowly, so the folks could absorb the meaning of the words. She turned here and there, gesturing for emphasis, just at the right times. For a moment, she felt as if she were Abraham Lincoln, speaking to the listeners at the dedication of the Pennsylvania battlefield, where brave young men, both Yankee and Confederate--some not much older than Henry--had fought and died.

Jeannie reached the end of her speech: "that this nation, under God, shall have a new birth of freedom; and that government of the people, by the people, for the people, shall not perish from the earth."

The room was stony silent, as Jeannie slowly returned from the Gettysburg Battlefield to the present. Then, above the thunderous applause, she heard Henry's piercing whistle. Her parents smiled with happiness and pride. And Mr. Markham and his cowboys shouted and clapped their hands loudly.

"Thank you, Jeannie," Pastor Thompson said, raising his hands to quiet the folks. "Nicely done, Jeannie.

You've made us all proud we're Americans, living in this wonderful country." Pastor Thompson paused a moment. Then he said, "While we're at it, let's remember the Alamo in San Antonio, and the brave men who died there, fighting for the freedom of Texas--Davy Crockett, Jim Bowie, and all the others--so that, today, as part of the United States, we can, now, seek our future in the great Lone Star State of Texas!"

That was it! Everyone in the room stood up and began cheering and shouting, "Remember the Alamo!"

Jeannie knew Pastor Thompson hadn't expected this. He raised his hands, and finally, it grew quiet. "Thank you, folks," he said--"but, let's not forget--we are in a house of God."

Glancing at one another sheepishly, the cowboys quickly seated themselves. Then Pastor Thompson hurried on, "I'm sure, we're all hungry by now. So, folks, let's go outside and enjoy the rest of our festivities."

Mrs. Lengenfeld and Helga sat with the Hansons at one of the picnic tables. Ma and Mrs. Lengenfeld opened the dinner baskets they'd prepared, while Pa, Henry, Mr. Markham, and his ranch hands sat at an adjoining table, waiting for the delicious food to be served.

Pastor Thompson and his wife joined Billy Joe's family. Several, other families sat near. After Pastor rose and gave the blessing, there was an excited chorus of laughing chatter, as folks enjoyed their meal of friend chicken, potato salad, and other tasty foods. For dessert, there were generous slices of blackberry or pecan pie.

After dinner the men pitched horseshoes. The young folks played tag and hide and go seek. When Jeannie was "It" in hide and go seek, she was surprised to find Helga and Billy Joe kneeling behind the same bush.

Helga was reading a red, heart-shaped paper. She looked up flustered. "Billy Joe just give me dis valentine," she explained softly.

Billy Joe's face turned as red as the valentine he'd given Helga.

"Oh," Jeannie gave an embarrassed reply. "That's nice," she murmured, feeling as if she'd interrupted a special moment.

Then recovering, she said, "You'd both better run fast and beat me to the oak tree before I get there, or you're both 'It'."

Billy Joe outran her and tagged in free, but Helga wasn't fast enough. She was "It" for the next game.

By the time the celebration ended, Mrs. Lengenfeld had given Helga permission to spend the night with Jeannie. Riding home at sunset, the girls dangled their feet over the back end of Pa's wagon.

Helga shyly reached in her pocket and gave Jeannie the red, heart valentine. "Billy Joe said he make up the verse, all by himself," she whispered.

"Really? I didn't know he could write verses."

"Me neither," Helga said. "It's nice vords."

Jeannie opened the valentine heart. Inside was a piece of tablet paper pasted to the bottom half of the heart. Printed in pencil, she read:

"Roses are red
Violets are blue
Helga, dear,
I'll always love you!"
Signed: Billy Joe

"Helga!" Jeannie gasped.

"Shh!" Helga hissed, glancing over her shoulder with a nervous giggle. "Ja, dot's vot he wrote me!" she whispered poking the valentine deep in the pocket of the apron, covering her best dress.

"Vell," she said, with a sigh, "maybe Billy Joe is not so bad after all."

Jeannie glanced at her best friend, sitting beside her. Helga's face seemed to have a special glow of contented happiness, as she stared off into the distance.

"Oh, well," Jeannie told herself. "Does a dog have fleas? Does a duck like water?" She shook her head and tried not to smile. Spring had sprung early, and love was in bloom!

Then she thought about her own special love for Diamond. Someday, she promised herself, probably for the hundredth time; someday, she'd have herself a big spread. She'd raise all kinds of beautiful, wonderful horses. And everyday, she and Diamond would ride together, as fast as the wind blowing across the prairie on a fine spring day.

"We'll be happy and carefree, just like those hawks flying up there in the sky," she told herself.

Chapter 16
“A Spring Baby”

February passed to March, and March became late April. The cultivated fields were green with young, growing things. As far as the eye could see, the prairie was a carpet of bluebonnets and colorful wild flowers.

Jeannie sniffed the warm air and smelled the fresh smell of new life pushing up through the soil. Tiny butterflies flittered around in the long, prairie grass. She was enjoying her afternoon walk home from school, down the dirt road to the Markham place with Helga. “School’s going to end May tenth,” Jeannie said.

“Ja, how fast the time vent.”

Jeannie squinted up at the cloudless sky and said, “Weather’s already starting out warm. I have a feeling we’re in for another hot summer.”

When the girls reached the trail to the Markham house, Jeannie said, “I think I’ll walk up with you, and then, I’ll just cut across the pasture to my house.”

“”Why not?” Helga said. “I like your company.”

Mr. Markham met the girls when they arrived. “Come on, ladies,” he said, “I have a surprise for you in the barn.”

“Oh, Mr. Markham,” Helga squealed, “is it time for the baby horse?”

“The colt has arrived a little early,” Mr. Markham said, as the girls stretched their legs to keep up with his long strides. “He’s a mighty fine, little horse, in spite of that.”

“Oh, I can’t vait to see him!” Helga cried.

Diamond’s foal! Jumping grasshoppers! Although she wanted to run, Jeannie forced herself to a quick walk.

In the shadowy barn, inside the first stall, they saw

him!

"Oh, grannies, Helga! Isn't he something!" Jeannie whispered, creeping closer.

"Look at his vobbly, little legs," Helga said softly. "He can hardly stand up."

"He was just born this morning," Mr. Markham explained, standing beside the hay-filled stall.

"He has a white tuft of diamond-shaped hair right in the same place as his pa," Jeannie observed. "And he's coal-black like him, too."

"Oh, look!" Helga squealed. "He's trying to nurse his mutter. Vatch how he nudges against her. He's such a hungry, little baby. See, the milk is dripping down his chin. You need a napkin, mister!" she scolded gently.

Susie leaned around and licked her son's shoulder. Then she moved a bit closer, so he could nurse more easily.

"You like your little son, eh, girl?" Mr. Markham asked. "Well, we'll leave you alone now, so y'all both can get some rest."

Outside the barn, Mr. Markham turned to Jeannie and said, "You know, Jeannie, the colt is Diamond's son, isn't he?"

She nodded and said, "He is, sure enough. Looks just like him."

"Well, I was wondering what you wanted to do with him?"

"Me?" Jeannie asked, puzzled.

"If he's Diamond's son, I was thinking you might want to have a say, as to what I should do with him." Mr. Markham gave a slight nod toward Helga. "Like, who should raise him--who should train him--who he should belong to."

"Well, sir," Jeannie said, playing along and acting confused, "He's Susie's son, too, Mr. Markham."

"That's true," Mr. Markham said, with a twinkle in his eyes. "But I was wondering if you had any ideas--about what we should do with him?" He twisted his gray mustache between his thumb and forefinger.

All this time Helga stood nearby, nervously biting her lower lip, waiting with her blue eyes sad-like and anxious.

"Hmm--," Jeannie said, in a puzzled way, dragging it out as long as she could. Helga looked first at Mr. Markham and then at Jeannie with her pleading eyes, "I think, maybe--we might as well give the feisty, little critter to Helga," Jeannie finished quickly.

Helga's face brightened like the sun. She looked at Mr. Markham, expectantly.

"Would you like to have the colt for your own, Helga?"

"Oh, ja, Mr. Markham," Helga said, jumping up and down with excitement. "He's a vonderful little colt."

"Well, then, he's yours," Mr. Markham said. "Susie needs a rest from a spry, young girl like you. I think you need a horse that can keep up with Diamond."

"Ja, dot vould be nice," Helga said. "Diamond is always having to vait for Susie and me."

"How about training the colt?" Mr. Markham asked.

"Oh, I can help Helga train him when he's ready, Mr. Markham. It took me awhile with Diamond, but we'll get it done," Jeannie said confidently. "I'll help her with the colt."

"Helga, you'll have to ride Susie for a spell, yet. I don't expect the colt will be ready for riding for quite some time," Mr. Markham said, as they strolled toward the house. "But when you've got him all trained up, he's yours to ride and take care of, too."

"Ja, I do it," Helga said gratefully. "Thank you, Mr. Markham. And tank you, Jeannie." She gave Jeannie a big hug. "I can't vait to start training my horse."

"All right," Mr. Markham said, untying Blackie from the porch railing. He mounted and said, "I've got to meet Slim and the boys. They're working on the fences in the south pasture."

"Bye, Mr. Markham," Jeannie said.

"Tank you very much, Mr. Markham," Helga called.

Mr. Markham turned in his saddle and tipped his hat to the girls.

"Such a good man," Helga said. "Mutter says he reminds her of Poppa. I wonder if he is lonely without a wife and children."

"He probably is lonesome," Jeannie said. "Since his wife died almost two years ago, Pa says he's kept a lot to himself. I remember Mr. and Mrs. Markham used to visit us often. I'd be in bed, but I could hear them laughing and talking and having a good time with my folks."

"He doesn't laugh too much now," Helga said. "Sometimes he laughs, when Mutter tells him to clean off his boots before coming in the house."

"Does he clean them off?"

"Ja, sure," Helga said smiling. "I tink he doesn't want to hear Mutter scolding him. He's a very nice man."

"Yes, he's Pa's best friend," Jeannie said.

Helga turned to Jeannie with a smile and said, "You are my best friend, too, Jeannie Ruth Hanson!"

"Thanks, Helga Marie Lengenfeld," Jeannie said, giving Helga a tight hug. "You're my best friend, too. So what are you going to name your new colt?"

"Hmm," Helga said thoughtfully, biting her lower lip. "He vas born this morning. I think, I call him--Morning Star."

"That's a pretty name, Helga," Jeannie said, with a nod of approval. "Morning Star is a perfect name for Diamond's little son."

Chapter 17
"Summer Fun"

"Well, class," Pastor Thompson said on May fifteenth, "have a pleasant summer. School is now officially ended until next September. You are excused to go home!"

With their final report cards tucked in their school satchels, Helga and Jeannie followed the rest of the kids outside. Everyone screamed loudly--just for the fun of it--as they all raced away, following different trails toward their homes.

Jeannie glanced back to see Pastor Thompson on the doorsteps with an arm over Mrs. Thompson's shoulders. They smiled and waved to her.

"Helga," Jeannie said, "turn around and wave."

Both girls waved goodbye. Billy Joe held back and waited for them to catch up. "When are we going swimming in the river?" he asked.

"I can't swim," Helga said.

"What?" Billy Joe asked, incredulously.

"That's right," Jeannie said. "I told her way back last summer, it was time she learned how to swim."

"Okay," Billy Joe said, "I know a perfect place in the river to teach Helga how to swim. It's like a shallow, little lake. It's protected by a border of rocks that keeps it away from the main current."

"Sure, I know that place," Jeannie said. "So what do you say, Helga? Want to learn how to swim?"

"Well, I try, but I vant you close by, Jeannie," she said.

"I'll be there," Jeannie said. "I'll ask Henry if he wants to go swimming with us. I'm pretty sure Pa will let him come. Do y'all want to go to the river tomorrow?"

"Okay with me," Billy Joe said.

"All right," Helga agreed.

"Henry and I will ride over for you, Helga. So have Susie ready," Jeannie instructed. "And Billy Joe, be at the river where the road meets the bridge at about noontime. And then, we can all go to that special swimming hole."

The next day Henry rode his horse Scout, Jeannie was astride Diamond, and Helga rode Susie.

Billy Joe waited at the bridge, sitting on his horse, Bright Eyes. "Follow me," he said, leading them south, down river. Riding single file, they followed the river, skirting along the upper bank, through thickets of cedars and oaks, past pecan trees, and scrubby patches of undergrowth.

Soon they reached a clearing where the riverbank dipped down and spread out into a shallow place with a sandy beach. "Yep, this is it," Jeannie said, slipping off Diamond's back.

"It's a good spot for you to learn to swim, Helga," Billy Joe said, helping her dismount.

"Jeannie, those cedars we passed, give off such a nice smell," Helga said.

"They sure do," Jeannie agreed. "I love to smell the cedar trees."

Henry untied the picnic basket on Scout's back and set it on the sand of a scooped-out ledge on the riverbank.

Jeannie knew the river sometimes overflowed its banks, in winter, when the water ran high. But, today, the little shore was an inviting, sandy place. Since the water would weigh heavy on them, when they were wet, everyone had worn lightweight overalls, cut off above the knees.

"Look!" Helga said, pointing to a thicket of berry bushes growing along the sandy bank. "Let's pick blackberries. Look how big dey are!"

Jeannie stared at the cluster of bushes, heavy with sweet fruit. "Yep, they're good and ripe. Real big and fat and black," she said. "I'll empty the chicken out of the lard bucket. We can use it." Jeannie dumped the fat pieces of fried chicken on a flower-sack dishtowel inside the picnic basket.

"Billy Joe," Henry said, nodding to the river, "let's you and me go for a swim, while the girls pick berries."

At the berry bushes, the girls immediately plopped a handful of fat, juicy berries into their mouths and let the juice run down their chins. It didn't matter today about berry juice stains. They knew they'd be going in the water soon, and even if the stains didn't come clean, they were wearing their oldest clothes, anyway.

"We better not eat any more," Jeannie soon said. "They could give us a bellyache."

"Ja, dot's true," Helga said. "But they taste so goot!"

After the girls had filled the lard bucket with berries and set it in the picnic basket, they strolled down to the river's edge and slowly stepped in the water. It seeped around their feet and legs. They waited until they grew accustomed to its coolness before wading in further.

"Come on out here. It's not that deep," Henry called, standing in water, chest high.

"Yeah, but don't forget, you're about six feet tall," Billy Joe said, moving toward the girls. "I'm about five feet, seven inches, and Helga is lucky if she measure five feet."

"Well, we're all here to help you learn to swim, right, Helga?" Henry said, smiling. "We won't let you drown."

Helga's teeth were beginning to chatter.

"Sink down in the water, where you are, until it reaches your neck," Billy Joe said, moving close to her. "Then you'll feel warmer."

Jeannie waded further out and treaded water in place. "Helga, it's nice, once you get used to it," she said.

Helga sank in the water until it touched her chin.

"Now, give me your hands," Billy Joe said, "and stretch out on your back like you're in bed. Keep your chin up and kick your feet. Hold your legs close and kind of stiff. Don't bend your knees."

Helga obeyed.

"That's right," Billy Joe said, pulling her toward him and taking tiny steps backward. "Now, don't splash the water so much with your feet. Just kind of kick gently, but stiff-legged."

Helga's feet pushed forward, as Billy Joe continued to step backward. "Good, Helga. That's it," he said softly. After a time he taught Helga to float. "Don't worry about getting water in your ears," he said. "It won't hurt you."

Jeannie turned over on her back and floated in water beside Helga. "This is fun, isn't it Helga?"

"Ja, it's nice," Helga said, squinting to protect her eyes, while the bright sunlight warmed her face.

"Just keep lying back and keep your legs stiff. If you can float," Jeannie said, "you won't ever drown. And it's a good way to rest your arms and legs when they get tired from swimming."

"Am I really floating?" Helga asked.

"Yes," Jeannie said, smiling. "Now, if you kick your feet, you can go most anywhere, even without moving your arms at your sides." Jeannie kicked herself closer to shore, and Helga followed with little churning kicks of her feet.

When the water became too shallow to float, they both tucked their feet under and sat down in the water.

"Um!" Helga said. "The water's varm here."

"It's always warmer close to shore," Jeannie said. "Look, Helga, the boys are having a water fight."

They watched the boys splash water on one another. Then Henry reached over and pushed Billy Joe's head under the water. Billy Joe bobbed up sputtering, but Henry had disappeared. Suddenly Billy Joe's legs buckled. He fell back in the water again.

"Henry just pushed Billy Joe at the back of his knees from underneath the water," Jeannie explained.

"I'll get you, Henry!" Billy Joe cried, diving under water.

Both boys came up laughing and sputtering. "Race you to the rocks up ahead," Billy Joe said.

"Let's go!" Henry shouted.

The girls watched them race toward the rocks. "Dey are really splashing a lot of water," Helga said.

"Sure are. They're churning the river into a white foam," Jeannie said, giggling. "They just love to act rowdy."

"I won!" Henry shouted, touching the boulder at the far end of the swimming hole.

"You have longer arms," Billy Joe said. "That's why you won." Then he turned and raced back toward the girls with Henry in hot pursuit.

"One more thing, Helga," Jeannie said, ignoring the boys, "just swish your hands around in the water, like this, and swing your legs around in the same place. It's called 'treading water'. That will keep you up, and you won't sink down."

Helga practiced staying afloat in the chest-high water.

"That's it, Helga," Jeannie said, watching her bob up and down. "Keep it up. You're treading water. Now, lie back and float."

"Doing good, Helga," Billy Joe said, swimming close. He stood up in the water. "Now, I'm going to teach you how to use both your arms and your legs, so that you will really know how to swim."

Helga stood upright in the waist-deep water and pushed two, wet braids over her shoulder. She listened carefully to Billy Joe.

"I want you to lie on your stomach in the water and kick your feet like I taught you. Begin to reach with your arms, one at a time, bringing them back down to your waist. Let your legs push you, and your arms pull you. Reach with one arm, pull back to your waist. Reach with the other arm, and repeat," he said, demonstrating the motions with his arms. "See how it done?"

Helga nodded. She bit her lower lip nervously.

"Remember to keep your knees stiff and paddle with your feet," Billy Joe said.

Helga took a deep breath.

"I'll stay in front of you, so you won't sink." Billy Joe smiled reassuringly. "And don't forget to breathe. Turn your head to the side and take in air through your mouth. Then blow it out slowly, with your face as close to the water as you can hold it, without swallowing water. Watch me."

Billy Joe put his face close to the water, opened his mouth, took in air, and slowly released it. "Now, let's try to swim," he said, reaching for Helga's hands.

"I try," Helga said, holding her chin out of the water, as she stretched out flat on her stomach.

"Kick," Billy Joe said.

Helga kicked, and Billy Joe led her forward. "Now breathe, and pull with your arms, and kick," he said, releasing her hands.

"Keep it up, Helga," Jeannie said, smiling happily. "You're swimming."

Helga was splashing the water. "Don't fight the water, Helga," Henry said, swimming beside her.

"Pull easy...kick easy...relax..."

Helga's strokes improved.

"Turn your face to the side and take in a breath with your mouth. Keep your face close to the water, as you breathe out," Billy Joe said, swimming beside her.

Helga crossed to the far end of the water and touched bottom with her feet. Gasping for breath and smiling at the same time, she stood up, brushing water from her eyes. "I do it!" she cried. "I do it."

"Yes, ma'am, Helga, you do it," Billy Joe said, patting her on the back.

"Good, Helga!" Jeannie said, swimming to her. "Now that you know how to swim, let's go back across together."

Helga stretched out forward and swam with Jeannie to the other side. After they had rested, Jeannie said, "This time, let's kick out feet and float back across."

When Henry and Billy Joe swam to deeper water to continue their water games, the girls climbed out on shore and sat in the warm sun, letting it dry their clothes.

"I have to keep practicing how to breathe and keep my face in the vater," Helga said. "But now, I'm starved! Swimming makes me hungry."

"Me, too," Jeannie said, reaching for the picnic basket. "Let's set out the dinner, so we can all eat."

After Henry and Billy Joe had eaten their fourth piece of chicken and two bowls of Ma's pinto beans with cornbread, they both leaned back in the sand and stretched out.

"Ohh!" Henry moaned. "I'm so full, I could bust!"

"Don't mention any more food to me," Billy Joe said. "I don't want to eat for a week!"

"Is that so?" Jeannie teased. "You mean, you don't want any peach cobbler pie? You want us girls to eat all the pie?"

"Well, no," Billy Joe said quickly. "But I don't want any just yet. I'm too full."

The girls hadn't quite finished their second piece of chicken, and their cornbread and beans. Helga turned to Billy Joe and said, "Young man, you eat too fast. You probably get a stomach-ache now."

"I hope not," he said, rubbing his middle.

"I think we should take a walk, after Helga and I put everything away," Jeannie said. "We could go exploring."

"Aw, there's not much more to see," Billy Joe said. "Me and my brothers usually just come here to this part of the river and swim."

"Well, let's see what's further down river," Henry

said. "Then we'll turn around and come back."

"All right by me," Billy Joe said. "As soon as I'm rested up."

Chapter 18
"An Interesting Discovery"

The little group plodded cautiously, single file through the dark, shadowy oaks and cedars along the riverbank, pushing through tangled vines and thick patches of undergrowth.

"I hope we don't find a snake in here," Helga said, chewing on her lip.

Jeannie didn't want to meet any snakes either, or another bobcat, and especially not a bear. From what Pa had told her, bears could still be found in the denser parts of the woods. She wouldn't mention that to Helga, though. Instead she said, "Going's getting rough, Henry. Maybe we should go back."

"Look!" Billy Joe said, crashing through the cedars and tangled brush up ahead. I think we're coming into another clearing."

"Yeah," Henry said. He pointed to a circle of rocks on the wide, sandy beach near the river's edge. "There's an old campfire."

"Yep, look at those black rocks inside it," Billy Joe said, drawing closer.

Henry stooped down and picked up a piece of black flint. "Must have been Comanches," he said. "See this flint stone. They use flint to make a fire."

"Jeannie, what's this?" Helga pointed to a chiseled piece of stone with a short, sharp point. "It looks like a black Christmas tree."

"Unhuh," Jeannie said, examining it. "That's an arrowhead. Indians used it on their arrows or their throwing spears to kill game, and sometimes, they used arrows and spears in their wars, too. Pa says most of them have rifles now. They don't use bows and arrows much anymore."

"I'm sure this was once a Comanche camp," Henry said. "Look at this piece of reed basket I found behind that small rock over there." He held up a braided strand of woven reed attached to a circular base.

"They carry water in buffalo-leather pouches. Some of their baskets are made like this," Henry said. "Sometimes they store nuts and berries in baskets."

"Ja, is that so?" Helga's eyes widened in appreciation. "Dey are very smart to live off the land like dot."

"Here's another arrowhead," Billy Joe said, holding up a sharp pointed, black, shiny arrowhead. It looks almost new. "You want it for a keepsake, Helga?"

"Ja, sure," Helga said gratefully. "Tank you, Billy Joe." She slipped the arrowhead into her pocket.

"We'd better go back now," Henry said, shading his face to the sky. "The sun's pretty far over in the west."

Leaving the abandoned Indian camp, Jeannie wondered whether it had once been the camp of the Comanches who had taken Diamond that frightening night last year. "Oh, grannies! I hope there aren't any Comanches around here now," she said, peering about in the darkening shadows of the woods.

"No, Pa told me many have gone down into Mexico," Henry said. "A few are still in the Palo Duro Canyon. Too many settlers coming into West Texas every month, especially, since the railroad has reached Abilene." He pushed a long vine out of their path. "Pa said, one of these days, the railroad might even pass by the trading post. Most Indians will be on reservation land by then."

"Well, in some ways, a railroad is good," Jeannie said, frowning, "And in some ways, it isn't. I don't know whether I'm going to like it, so much, when this place fills up with people."

Reaching the picnic area, the group untied their waiting horses. "I need plenty of ranch land, if I'm going to have a horse ranch when I grow up," she complained grumpily.

Henry ruffled the back of her head. "Aw, now, Shorty," he said, "don't worry none about that. There'll be plenty of land left in West Texas for you to have your horse ranch."

"Maybe," Jeannie said, mounting up. "I'm going to be mighty disappointed if there isn't. Diamond and I are counting on it, aren't we, boy?" She patted Diamond's neck affectionately. As usual--when she spoke to Diamond--he bobbed his head up and down. Jeannie smiled and patted him again.

The boys rode ahead, while Helga and Jeannie rode side by side. "Tank you for helping me learn to swim, Jeannie," Helga said.

"It was fun," Jeannie said. "You learned fast, and I'm glad you did. You need to know how to swim out here in this wild country."

"Ja, I'm glad I learned, too. Mutter will be proud of me." Helga turned and smiled at Jeannie. "I know I said it before, but I say it again. You are my best friend, Jeannie."

"You're my best friend, too, Helga," Jeannie said, smiling back.

"And I'll come and visit you some day, when you

get dot horse ranch you keep telling me about," Helga said, with a teasing grin.

"And I'll ride Diamond, and you'll ride Morning Star," Jeannie said, caught up in her dream. "We'll go riding all over my horse ranch."

"Ja, we'll do dot. It's a promise," Helga said solemnly. "Jeannie, let's be friends forever."

"Yes," Jeannie agreed softly, looking across to Helga. "Friends forever and ever, Helga. You can count on it!"

Chapter 19
"Exciting News"

"Ole Blue, let's go visit Helga and see what she's doing today," Jeannie said, sitting on the front porch steps after her morning chores were done. "I'll saddle up Diamond, and we'll go over there. Do you want to go play with Lady?"

"Woof!" Ole Blue barked. He wiggled and licked her hand.

"So you understand, do you?" Jeannie giggled. "You want to go visiting, too?"

Ole Blue wagged his tail and barked again.

"Okay, let's go get Diamond," Jeannie said. "But first, I'll ask Ma if it's all right to go visiting today."

When Jeannie and Diamond approached the Markham ranch house, Lady greeted them, barking happily. Helga hurried outside. "I'm so glad to see you today," she said, waiting patiently for Jeannie to finish tying Diamond's reins to the hitching rail. "Come, let's sit in the swing. I have some vonderful news to tell you." She took Jeannie's arm and pulled her to the porch swing.

Ole Blue and Lady dashed away in their favorite game of chase. Jeannie plopped down on the porch swing and asked, "What is it Helga? You're so excited."

"Ja, I'm excited, Jeannie," Helga squealed. "Guess what?" She paused and lowered her voice to a dramatic whisper. She leaned in closer and said, "Mama and Mr. Markham--they are getting married!"

"Really!" Jeannie exclaimed, hugging her friend.

"Ja, really," Helga said, nodding her head. "They told me this morning."

"Well, jumping grasshoppers!" Jeannie exlaimed.

"Isn't that wonderful! Mr. Markham is a nice man, and your ma is a very sweet lady." Then with a concerned look in her eyes, Jeannie turned to her friend and asked, "Seriously, Helga, is it REALLY all right with you?"

"Ja, sure," Helga said. "My papa died when I was a little girl. Now, Mutter is so happy. Her eyes just shine. She and Mr. Markham are always laughing these days."

"I'm happy for you and for your Ma," Jeannie said, hugging her friend.

With a giggle, Helga said, "Mr. Markham tells me, now, I am his little girl."

"Well, you will be soon," Jeannie said. "And now, we'll always be neighbors. Sometimes, I used to wonder what I would do if your ma and you ever left Mr. Markham's ranch and moved somewhere else to live."

"We never move away," Helga promised, squeezing Jeannie's hand.

"When will they get married?" Jeannie asked. She gave the swing a little push with her foot.

"Mutter asked me if I would like for them to get married two months from now on my birthday in July. I said that would be vonderful," Helga said, as the swing rocked gently. "She wants me to be a bridesmaid, and she wants you to be a bridesmaid, too! She's going to ask your mutter to be Matron of Honor, and Mr. Markham vants your poppa to be his Best Man."

"Oh grannies, Helga, what fun!" Jeannie cried, lost in her thoughts, as she imagined the happy day. "Won't that be nice. It's going to be a wonderful wedding!"

"Oh, ja, and Mutter is going to make her dress. She's going to make a long dress for me, too."

"You'll be beautiful," Jeannie said, imagining Helga in a long dress with her pretty, white hair touching her waist.

"And you'll be beautiful, too," Helga said, as the swing came to a stop. "Mr. Markham and Mutter are going over to visit your mutter and poppa today and tell them the news. Then she'll ask your mutter to be in the wedding, and they will make plans. Mutter is hoping they will do it."

"Oh, I'm sure Ma and Pa will want to be in the wedding," Jeannie said. "They love Mr. Markham and your ma."

Just as Jeannie had expected, Ma and Pa were almost as excited as she was, to get to be in the wedding. The news soon spread throughout the neighboring ranches. Everyone was planning to attend the Frank Markham and Emma Lengenfeld wedding celebration on Sunday, July 4, 1885.

"Be still, dear," Ma said, holding several pins in her hand, as she began tucking the hem of Jeannie's powder blue, floor-length dress.

Jeannie stood very still on the kitchen table, so that Ma could pin the exact length evenly.

"Now, turn slowly, just a bit, dear," Ma instructed.

Turning, Jeannie glimpsed her reflection in the kitchen window. Grannies! It was such a pretty dress, and it was exactly like Helga's. They would both wear blue dresses with puffed sleeves and a white lace trim around the neck that dipped into a "V". There was also white lace around the hem of each dress.

"I guess I'm going to have to learn to sew one of these days, Ma," Jeannie said, resolutely. "It sure does come in handy."

"Yes, it does, dear," Ma said.

Jeannie breathed a heavy sigh. "I think, Ma, I'm beginning to grow up. I'll be fourteen in November. It's about time for me to learn how to cook and sew."

"You sound so mournful about it, Jeannie." Ma chuckled. "It can be fun. Maybe you won't have as much time for Diamond, but there will be plenty of play-time left."

"My dress is beautiful, Ma. Thank you for making it."

"You and Helga are going to be as pretty as a pair of bluebonnet flowers," Ma said, giving Jeannie her hand. "You can step down now."

Jeannie stepped lightly on the cane-bottom chair and then to the floor. She slipped the dress over her head carefully and pulled on her overalls and shirt.

"Now, I'll put in the hem and press your dress. And it will be finished," Ma said. "Then I have to work on mine."

"Ma, do you want me to press my dress?"

"No, dear, I wouldn't want that heavy, black iron to get too hot. It might scorch the dress. I'd better do it this time. But there is some family ironing to do."

"I'll do it after you press my dress," Jeannie said.

"Thank you, dear. That will be a big help," Ma said, giving Jeannie a quick peck on her cheek.

Chapter 20
"Wedding Joy"

Jeannie turned the doorknob slowly and peeked through the door of the Young People's, Sunday School room where Mrs. Lengenfeld, Ma, Helga, and she waited. The sanctuary was something to see! The church was filled with folks all dressed up in their best clothes.

"Psst! Helga," Jeannie whispered. "Come and look."

Helga put her face next to Jeannie's and peeked out at the crowded auditorium. "Oh, Jeannie, the ladies look so pretty in their flowered dresses with all those bright colors."

Jeannie nodded and put her hand over her mouth, so she wouldn't giggle out loud. "And the men look so stiff in their dark suits with their hair all slicked back and parted in the middle," she whispered. "See how nice their beards and moustaches are trimmed, and Mr. Markham's ranch hands are all dressed up, too."

"Ja, I see," Helga said softly. "Look at Billy Joe, dressed so nice, sitting with his folks."

"Unhuh, everyone looks all polished and perky!"

"Girls," Ma said, "remember when you see Pa and Mr. Markham standing at the altar, Mrs. Thompson will begin playing, and it will be your turn to walk in. Try to walk slowly and hold your bouquet of flowers close to your tummies."

"Yes, ma'am," Jeannie said. "Oh, I see them, now. Mr. Markham and Pa are standing on the right side of the altar. They're looking our way. Mrs. Thompson is playing the pump organ for us to come."

Jeannie glanced at Helga. Both girls breathed in deeply.

"Ja, I'm ready," Helga said. Ma opened the door for the girls. Holding her bouquet of mixed prairie flowers, Helga walked slowly up the aisle in time to the organ music.

Jeannie followed a few steps behind, thinking how pretty Helga looked, floating along like a princess in her powder blue dress with her wavy, white hair touching her waist.

"Drink to me only, with thine eyes...." Jeannie hummed the lovely bridal melody, as she tried to still the fast beating of her heart. She joined Helga on the left side of the altar. Pa gave the girls a quick wink. Mr. Markham, looking a little pale, gave them a nervous smile.

The girls turned and watched Ma coming toward them. Jeannie's heart swelled with loving pride. Ma looked so beautiful! Her black, wavy hair was pinned neatly in a bun, and her full skirted, yellow, crinoline dress rustled with each tiny step. She carried a large bouquet of pretty, red roses that seemed to blend with the pink glow on her cheeks.

Jeannie remembered Mrs. Lengenfeld had planted a rose garden shortly after her arrival from Germany. It was nice this year, that the roses were all in bloom, just in time for her wedding bouquet. And there were enough roses for Ma's lovely bouquet, as well.

When Ma was standing beside Jeannie and Helga, Mrs. Thompson's pump organ rang out with the first chords of the wedding march melody. Jeannie murmured the first line to herself, "Here comes the bride...."

Everyone rose, and all heads turned to watch the

bride. Jeannie gasped with delight. Oh grannies! She would remember this moment always, as pretty, golden haired Emma Lengenfeld began her slow walk in a beautiful, ecru-colored, floor-length dress, decorated with touches of light blue, crocheted lace. At her lace-collared throat, she wore an ivory broach showing a lovely, portrait bust of a lady. Mrs. Lengenfeld had told the girls earlier that the broach had once belonged to her mother.

Woven in her hair was a crown of mixed flowers. A few blue ribbon streamers touched the braided bun at the nape of her neck, while other longer ones touched the hem of her long dress.

Mr. Markham's foreman, Slim, escorted Mrs. Lengefeld. As Jeannie watched them approaching, she could see, Slim looked simply grand in his black boots and pants. At the collar of his white, starched shirt a black, string tie made a perfect bow. His lean face was clean-shaven, and his long, brown hair had recently been trimmed to his neckline.

With flushed cheeks and bright blue eyes, Mrs. Lengenfeld smiled a beautiful smile and nodded occasionally to folks lining either side of the aisle. Yes, Jeannie decided, Mrs. Lengenfeld's bouquet of baby-pink roses added the perfect touch to making her a vision of downright loveliness!

Jeannie saw Mr. Markham swallow a few times. His Adam's apple bobbed up and down as Mrs. Lengenfeld joined him at the altar. She put her right hand on his left arm. Then the happy couple faced Pastor Thompson, standing before them with his Bible open, ready to began the wedding ceremony.

Chapter 21
"Future Plans and Lady's Surprise"

"Girls, you want some lemonade?" Helga's mother asked.

"Ja, Mutter, that would be nice," Helga said, giving the porch swing a little push with her toes. "It's so hot today."

"Thank you, Mrs. Lengenfeld. Oh grannies! I mean, Mrs. Markham," Jeannie said quickly, reddening, as she corrected herself. She lifted her feet, so Helga could continue to push them both.

"That's all right," Mrs. Markham said. "Both names are goot names. I'll bring you some lemonade now."

After Mrs. Markham entered the house, Jeannie said, "Your ma seems so happy."

"She is very happy," Helga said. "And Mr. Markham, I mean Poppa. You know, he asked me to call him 'Poppa', so I do that now."

Jeannie nodded.

"Poppa, he's smiling all the time when he's in the house. And you know what? He's getting a little, fat tummy. He says Mutter is feeding him too good." Helga laughed.

"I know. He is putting on pounds," Jeannie said. "He's going to have to stop eating so many of your ma's doughnuts."

"That's the truth," Helga nodded. "And now that we are talking about weight, I've been watching Lady. She is getting very fat!"

"Is that so?" Jeannie asked

Helga nodded and said, "The past few weeks she has gotten fat and lazy. She doesn't want to run much anymore."

"Helga, I think Lady is going to have puppies."

"You tink so?"

"And I'm sure they're Ole Blue's puppies, too," Jeannie said with a grin. "Those two have been thick as bees on a honeycomb. Besides, Ole Blue is the only hound dog around here. So he has to be the daddy."

"Have some lemonade," Mrs. Markham said, returning to the porch. She gave the girls each, a tall glass.

"Thank you, Mrs. Markham," Jeannie said.

"You're velcome," Mrs. Markham said, turning to go back inside.

"Blue!" Jeannie called. "Lady, come here."

Ole Blue appeared from around the corner of the house, followed by a slower Lady.

"Yes," Jeannie said, "Lady is going to have puppies; and soon, from the looks of her fat belly." Jeannie turned to her dog and said, "Blue, you're going to be a daddy any day. Isn't that something!" Blue licked her hand and wagged his tail.

"Maybe we have to marry the dogs to each other now," Helga said smiling. "Maybe we have another wedding!"

Jeannie giggled, "Oh, Helga, I don't know whether I could take another wedding this soon, Your ma's wedding was beautiful, and there was so much delicious food, too."

"It was beautiful," Helga replied. "I will never forget that wedding. Someday, I hope, I have a beautiful wedding."

"You will, Helga," Jeannie said confidently. "You'll be a beautiful bride."

"Thank you, Jeannie. Vot about you? Do you want

to get married someday?"

"Well, I expect, I won't be getting married any too soon." Jeannie said. "I have to get my horse ranch first. I have a lot to do before I get married. Maybe, I won't even get married. Maybe, I'll just live alone and raise my horses."

"Oh my, Jeannie," Helga said sadly, "you would get too lonesome all by yourself."

"Well, maybe," Jeannie said, sipping her lemonade, "but you could always come and visit me."

"Ja, I do that," Helga said smiling.

Chapter 22
"A Time of Sadness"

"Rain sure has come down hard," Jeannie told herself, gazing out her bedroom window at the dark, gloomy sky. "It's finally stopped after two days. I'm sure the creek is full, and no telling how high the river is."

She wondered what Helga was doing. It'd been over a week since she'd visited her. Did Lady have her puppies yet? And where was Ole Blue? He'd taken off on his own just before it started raining, and he hadn't come back home for two days.

Maybe he was over at the Markham's ranch waiting for Lady to have her pups. Well, he wouldn't know that she was going to have pups, but still, where could he be? It wasn't like him to stay away so long.

"Jeannie," Ma said softly, from the doorway. Her face was ashen. "Pa wants to talk to you. He's in the kitchen."

"Is anything wrong, Ma?" Jeannie asked anxiously.

Ma brushed a tear from her eye. "Hurry, dear. Pa's waiting."

Jeannie rushed into the kitchen to find Pa. Henry sat across from him at the table, staring down at the tablecloth. Pa's face was grim.

"Pa, you want to talk to me?" Jeannie asked, nervously twisting a strand of loose hair around her finger, while her heart pounded a fast drumbeat.

"Sit down, Punkin," Pa said, motioning to the chair beside him. "Punkin, I have real bad news."

"Bad news, Pa?"

"Yes, sweetheart," Pa took a deep breath. "It's not easy for me to tell you this, Punkin," he said softly. "Ole Blue is dead."

"What! Ole Blue?" Jeannie's voice quavered. She trembled all over. "Ole Blue?"

"Yes, Punkin," Pa said, putting his arms around Jeannie and holding her head against his chest. "Ole Blue has died and gone to heaven."

"No," Jeannie sobbed. "Not Ole Blue," she cried. "What happened, Pa? How did it happen?"

Pa stroked Jeannie's hair and waited until her sobs lessened. "He was a brave dog, Punkin, a very brave dog," Pa said gently. "He was so brave, he tried to kill a big rattler twice his size, and he did, too. But the rattler bit him a few times when he was fighting it. We found the dead rattler laying beside Ole Blue's body; and, he was a powerful big one, too."

"A rattler!" Jeannie sobbed. "A big one? Was it over there in the pasture by the Leon River?"

Pa nodded and said, "Yes, Punkin, that's where we found him."

"Oh, Pa, it must have been the same rattler that tried to strike Diamond," Jeannie wailed, tears spilling from her eyes. "Helga and I were riding with the dogs over there, just before cotton-picking time. He was a really big rattler, too."

Jeannie brushed away tears and went on in a shaky voice. "Ole Blue was going to try and kill him, right then, but I called him back, and we got out of there in a hurry!"

Jeannie sighed sadly, "Oh grannies! I should have told you about that rattler, Pa," she said. "Maybe you could've gone back and killed him. And Ole Blue would still be here with us." Jeannie shook her head and choked back more tears.

"Well, sweetheart," Pa said slowly, "God works in

mysterious ways, and we don't always understand His timing of things." Reaching in a side pocket of his overalls, Pa pulled out his handkerchief and gave it to her.

Jeannie wiped her eyes. "Oh, Pa," she moaned, in a fresh stream of tears, "what am I going to do without Ole Blue?"

"I'll miss him too, Punkin," Pa said softly. "That's a fact, for shore."

"And I'll miss him, Shorty," Henry said, in a voice so full he could hardly speak.

"We'll all miss him," Ma said, gently, drawing her chair in closer to Jeannie and Pa. "He was a real, good dog; and, sweetheart, I know for sure, God has a wonderful place for him, right now, in heaven." Ma kissed Jeannie's forehead and held her hand.

"You know, dear," Ma said, "The Bible tells us, in heaven, our loved ones are well and whole again." Ma looked into Jeannie's eyes. "I'm sure Ole Blue's spirit is up there right now, just barking and carrying on."

Then Ma smiled and said, "I imagine he's having a great time. Why, he's probably licking an angel's hand, like he used to do yours."

Jeannie grinned through her tears. "Do you really think so, Ma? Ole Blue licking on an angel's hand?"

"I'm sure of it," Ma said gently.

"Punkin, Henry and I done buried Ole Blue down by the creek where he liked to chase jack rabbits," Pa said. " We'll take you there, in a little while, if you want to go put some flowers on his grave."

Jeannie nodded. "Yes, Pa, I want to do that."

"I'll help you gather up a bouquet," Ma said, giving Jeannie a hug. "We have pretty wildflowers growing behind the house."

There was just a little sunlight left when Jeannie knelt beside the freshly dug mound of dirt. She carefully put the glass-filled jar of buttercups and prairie zinnias upright at the head of the grave. Pa, Ma, and Henry stood a little to the side, giving Jeannie her private moments alone with Ole Blue.

"Goodbye, dear friend," Jeannie whispered, as fresh tears streamed down her cheeks. "And, Dear God, I'm asking You to please take care of Ole Blue and keep him in Your loving care."

As Jeannie slowly rose, Ma put her arms around her, and they walked back to the house.

Chapter 23
"There is So Much to Do?"

"Jeannie! Jeannie!"

Someone was calling. Jeannie ran to the front door and opened it. "Howdy, Mr. Markham," she said, greeting their neighbor. "Please, come in." Jeannie held the door open.

"Jeannie, I want to take you to see Lady's new babies," Mr. Markham said, with a smile. He stepped into the parlor. "They look just like their daddy!"

"Ole Blue?"

"That's right," Mr. Markham said, twisting his gray moustache happily. "Ole Blue, sure enough, left us something to remember him by! His pups are already over a week old and wiggling and squirming around their ma. They're acting just like Ole Blue used to--moving and jumping around everywhere."

Mr. Markham removed his hat and went on, "I didn't come sooner, because we wanted to give you some time alone to think about Ole Blue. But today, Helga and I were thinking that you're about ready to come over and see his pups."

"Morning, Frank," Ma said, coming from the kitchen. "So Lady's had her pups?"

"Yes, Ruthie. They're past a week old. We thought Jeannie might like to come over and see them."

Jeannie nodded. "Yes sir, I'd sure enough like to see Ole Blue's pups. Is it all right if I go with Mr. Markham now, Ma?"

"Of course, dear," Ma said.

"I was thinking she might like to spend the night with Helga," Mr. Markham said. "And I'll bring her back tomorrow when she's ready to come home."

"Could I, Ma?"

"Go get your things," Ma said. "Matthew's working down at the barn, Frank. If you'd like, you can go down there and talk to him while you wait for Jeannie," Ma suggested. "He'll be glad to see you."

"Sure enough," Mr. Markham said. "I'll go see what he's doing."

It wasn't long before Helga took Jeannie by the hand and led her, into the back part of the kitchen, to the open pantry. There, on an old quilt, Lady lay beside four squirming puppies.

"Oh, grannies! Aren't they precious!" Jeannie cried, kneeling beside Lady. "And they do look just like Ole Blue. They all have his long ears and his big feet!"

"Ja, they look like their daddy, all right," Helga agreed.

"Do you think Lady would let me hold one?" Jeannie asked.

Helga nodded and said, "I hold the babies all the time."

Jeannie lifted a tiny pup and held him in the palm of her hands. "Listen, Helga," Jeannie whispered. "He's making little mewing sounds like a baby kitten."

She held the puppy close to her face. His tiny, pink tongue reached out and licked her cheek. "He's kissing me, Helga!" Jeannie squealed happily. "Just like Ole Blue."

"Ja, that one likes to lick your hands and face," Helga said, giggling. "Jeannie, I think you should take that one home with you when he's through nursing his mutter."

"He is cute, isn't he?" Jeannie said, scratching

behind his ears. The puppy opened his mouth in a wide yawn and settled down in her hands and closed his eyes. "He likes me scratching behind his ears," Jeannie said. "Look, now, he wants to sleep." She put the puppy down beside the other, little puppies. They were sprawled out on their bellies, nursing against Lady's full teats.

"There are four puppies," Helga said. "That's a lot." She sighed thoughtfully, as she and Jeannie left the room. "I vant to keep one for Lady, and you should have one," she said. "Maybe, you should have two, Jeannie. They could be friends together, just like Lady and her puppy I'll keep for her."

"Yes," Jeannie said. "That would be fun to have two puppies. They'd sure keep me busy, running around, looking after them."

"Now, we have one puppy left," Helga said, thoughtfully. "What should we do with him? Who could we give him to?"

"Well," Jeannie said with a grin, as the girls reached the front porch and sat down on the swing. "I think, maybe, Billy Joe might like a pup."

Helga's face reddened. She sat beside Jeannie and pushed the swing with a free foot. "You think so?"

"Does a bear like honey?" Jeannie asked. "Of course, he'd like to have one of Ole Blue's pups," Jeannie said. "You can ask him when we go to church on Sunday."

"Sure, I will do that." For a moment, Helga was thoughtful as the swing rocked forward and back. Then she stopped it with her toe and looked at her friend. "Jeannie, I never got to say it until today, but I'm truly sorry about Ole Blue."

"I miss him something awful," Jeannie said with a heavy sigh. "He was a good friend. Next time you come over to visit, I'll take you to his grave, and we can put some flowers on it. Pa buried him in the pasture down by the creek where he liked to run and play so much. He was always chasing after one critter or another."

Helga gave Jeannie a little hug. "Ja, we do that soon," she said. "You know, Jeannie, to tell the truth, I don't like to think about dying. First, I lose my papa, and now, we lose Ole Blue."

Jeannie nodded. "I just don't know what people do, when they lose loved ones, and they don't love God. They don't have any hope of ever seeing them again. But Ma said, she guessed Ole Blue was up in heaven, right now, having fun with the angels."

"She said that?" Helga asked, with a giggle.

"Even though I was so sad, when Ma said that, I had to laugh a little, because I thought it was funny," Jeannie said. She smiled and added, "I can just see Ole Blue running around in heaven and jumping up and licking the faces of angels."

"I know he's having a good time up there," Helga said. "And now, Jeannie, you will have two of Ole Blue's pups to love and take care of. They are acting just like their papa."

"They sure are," Jeannie agreed. "You know, Helga, I was thinking. So much has happened in just one year. Some things were bad, but God made everything turn out all right, like the time, I thought I'd lost Diamond forever when he was stolen, but we got him back. And another good thing happened soon after that. You came from Germany to live in Texas, and now, we're best friends."

Helga gave Jeannie's arm an affectionate squeeze. "And you taught me how to ride Susie," she said, remembering along with Jeannie.

"Thank the Lord, we all lived through that awful cyclone. And Diamond saved you and me and the dogs from the rattler. I--sure enough--will never forget the time Diamond saved me from that old bobcat. That critter was trying to kill both of us!"

"That's right," Helga said. "And I will never forget how you saved me from almost drowning, and later on, Henry and Billy Joe and you taught me how to swim. And soon, you will teach me how to train Diamond and Susie's little cold, Morning Star."

"Colt, Helga, colt!" Jeannie said, smiling.

"Ja, colt."

Jeannie lay her head against the back of the swing and said, "Remember how Billy Joe was always teasing you, and then, on Valentine's Day, he gave you a pretty card?"

"I remember," Helga said softly, as her cheeks turned pink.

"I know you still have the card in your little treasure box on your dresser," Jeannie whispered, smiling mischievously.

"Well, it's a pretty card," Helga said shyly, biting her lip. "Now, let's think of something else we remember."

'Okay," Jeannie said, seeing Helga's embarrassment. "I remember your ma's and Mr.

Markham's wonderful wedding on your birthday, and we got to be bridesmaids."

Helga smiled and said, "Afterward, there were all those colorful fireworks to remember America's Independence Day, July 4, 1776." She rushed on, "And Mr. Markham, I mean, Poppa, said every Fourth of July, we vill have a big celebration for three reasons; his and Mutter's wedding anniversary, my birthday, and America's Independence Day."

"Jumping grasshoppers! That will be such fun!" Jeannie exclaimed, giving Helga a hug. "I can't wait for July Fourth to come around again!"

"Oh, ja, you can," Helga said confidently. "But right now, you have to raise two of Ole Blue's pups. Have you thought of a name for them?"

"Well, I think I'll call the frisky one, Ole Blue, Junior," Jeannie said. "And the other one, I'll have to think about."

"Sure, Junior--that's a good name," Helga said, leaving the swing. "Let's go back inside and play with Lady's and Ole Blue's babies."

Jeannie knelt beside Lady's blanket and leaned back on her heels. She reached for the wiggliest of the four puppies. "Come here, Junior," she said, lifting him and holding him close to her cheek. Just as she expected, the puppy's tiny, pink tongue immediately reached out and began licking her face.

"You're just like your daddy, little feller," Jeannie said, scratching behind his ears while he licked her fingers. She felt something on her knees. Another baby puppy was struggling to climb up on her legs.

Jeannie giggled and sighed. "Thank You, God," she said gratefully, "for sending Helga and me Ole Blue's puppies."

"Ja, thank You, God," Helga said.

"I'll always miss Ole Blue, Helga," Jeannie said, lifting the puppy that was trying to climb on her legs. "But now that his puppies are here, they need care."

"That's true," Helga agreed, picking up a puppy and planting a little kiss on its tiny cheek.

Suddenly Jeannie's heaviness disappeared. Summer was almost over, and there was so much to be done! She had to train two baby puppies, and soon, she had to think about helping Helga train Morning Star.

"Well now, look here, Junior," Jeannie said softly, holding a puppy in each hand close to her face, "your cute, little sister wants some attention, too. So, you're just going to have to learn to share."

Grannies! There was so much to do. And another thing, she promised herself, from now on, she was going to spend more time with Ma in the kitchen learning how to cook. Helga's Ma was already teaching Helga some of her favorite German recipes. Maybe she and Helga could learn to crochet and knit. Why, they might even learn how to sew!

The rest of the summer promised busy days ahead. It was time to get started. And, one of the very first things she had to do was think of a name for Ole Blue's precious, little daughter.

SUMMARY OF JEANNIE, A TEXAS FRONTIER GIRL, Book 2.

In JEANNIE, A TEXAS FRONTIER GIRL, Book 2, the girls find their summer filled with puppies and a new colt to train. What is the name of Ole Blue's little daughter? Womanly skills, such as cooking and sewing, are part of the girls' activities. Soon, they share adventures with school friends. Will they help a family in need? Unexpected romance blooms for Helga at a Christmas party. What does Billy Joe have to do with it? Why is Jeannie considering Slim as a possible ranch foreman for her "someday" horse ranch? Why does he annoy her? Will Helga recover from a serious illness? Who is saved from a terrible snowstorm? Does her bitter attitude change when Jeannie meets a Comanche Indian family and their small children? There is unexpected money for Jeannie. Can it be used to buy her "someday horse ranch?" Who has a new baby? Who is gored by a long horn cow?

Be sure and look for JEANNIE, A TEXAS FRONTIER GIRL, BOOK 2, and follow more exciting adventures of two best friends, Jeannie and Helga, as they continue to grow up on the West Texas frontier of the 1880's.

Printed in the United States
88781LV00003B/88/A

9 781588 517050